The Secret Shelter

Sandi LeFaucheur

Brown Barn Books
Weston, Connecticut

Brown Barn Books,
a division of Pictures of Record, Inc.
119 Kettle Creek Road, Weston, Connecticut 06883, U.S.A.
www.brownbarnbooks.com

THE SECRET SHELTER

Library of Congress Control Number: 2004105925
ISBN: 0-9746481-4-0

LeFaucheur, Sandi

The Secret Shelter: a novel by Sandi LeFaucheur

Printed in the United States of America

If I'd Known Then . . .

If I'd known then what I know now—If I'd known then what I know now—

The words pounded through my head to the rhythm of the train wheels.

If I'd known then what I know now . . .

But when was *then* and when was *now?* Everything was back to front, topsy-turvy. Now was dull, dismal December 1940. Then—two months ago—had been sunny June 2002.

The train stopped at a nameless village. All the signs had been taken down in case the Germans invaded. I could have told them there would be no invasion and that I knew how the war would end. It was a bit like reading the last page of a book before the middle. I was stuck in the middle of the book now.

If I'd known then what I know now . . . I certainly wouldn't have agreed to take part in that history assignment. I thought back to how it had all started . . .

CHAPTER 1

⟫⟫⟫ June, 2002

I jerked out of my daydream and back to the here and now as the eraser whizzed past my left ear and plopped softly against the wall behind me. The class snickered. I looked down to hide my burning face behind a curtain of mouse-colored hair.

"Sophie Pinkerton, if you spent as much time here as you do in Cloud Cuckoo-Land, maybe your test scores would be better." Mr. Schmidt gave a sigh of annoyance. It was no easy task maintaining order in a classroom bursting at the seams with kids who didn't want to be there. His voice softened a bit. "Have you heard one word of what I've said? I have been explaining to the class the history assignment. You are to work in groups of three or four and get information about how the Second World War affected this area of South London."

"Information! Ve vant information, *ja?*" croaked carrot-topped Nathan Quigley, in a fake German accent.

"Very funny, Quigs. Perhaps you would like to work with Sophie and, say, Marina Curtis?"

"No way!" Quigs winked at Marina, who grinned back. Everyone liked Marina—the girls because she was clever and nice, and the boys because she was gorgeous, with raven hair and emerald eyes.

I, on the other hand, was not so popular. Mum said I was pretty, but then mothers are biased. And I, Miss Pudding-Face, spent most of my life daydreaming about Mr. Schmidt—tall and blond, with a heavenly German accent.

Marina leaned back in her chair and nudged me, breaking into my latest fantasy. She smiled broadly, pushing her glasses further up her perfect nose. "Well, at least I have you, Sophie. Shame we're stuck with Quigs. I have a brilliant idea. Mr. Schmidt said there's an air-raid shelter under the lawn in front of the school. Well, why don't we excavate it and see what's down there? There might be all sorts of stuff left behind from the war."

"Bodies! Dead bodies from the war. Ratatatatatatat!" Quigs sprayed an imaginary machine gun around the room.

"Not bodies," replied Marina witheringly. "But they might have left books, or comics, stuff like that."

"But . . . excavate it? Like, dig it up? Where would the door be? And Miss Pratt would never let us dig up the lawn, anyway."

Miss Pratt, the head teacher, ran the school like an army regiment. She was a stickler for neatness, and I certainly couldn't imagine her allowing us to desecrate the perfectly manicured lawn.

Marina's eyes sparkled as her enthusiasm grew. "Not the whole lawn, silly. Only where the door would be. Come on, there are lots of old people around who lived here in Penge or Beckenham during the war and who went to this school. They would be sure to remember where the entrance to the shelter was and how much dirt was put on top of it. Oh, do say yes. We could get heaps and heaps of extra credit for originality."

I found myself carried away by Marina's excitement and, heaven knows, I really needed help with my mediocre marks.

"Mr. Martin, my dad's neighbor, told me he went to this school during the war when it was just for boys," I said. "I'm sure he'd remember where the entrance to the shelter was. We could ask him."

Quigs put his head on the desk and snored loudly. Opening one eye, he gave the type of enlightened comment we had come to expect from him. "Boring. Just wake me up when you find a body."

❱ ❱ ❱

Mr. Martin hadn't seemed at all pleased about our plans to excavate the shelter, which surprised me. Most old people I knew liked nothing better than to talk about the past, particularly the war. But Dad said Mr. Martin had always struck him as a bit strange, sort of "lights on but nobody home," as Dad's new wife, Sylvia, put it. I didn't agree with that description. Mr. Martin had the most incredibly piercing pale blue eyes that looked right through you. I was sure he was definitely all there. Anyway, I had wheedled, pleaded, cajoled, and plied him with pound cake until he'd agreed to help us.

We must have made a curious sight—a shabby old man, two teachers, and three students staring intently at the grassy bank, as if we expected the lawn to rise up and take off like a flying saucer from the semi-circular driveway surrounding it.

Mr. Martin's pale blue eyes gazed at the lawn. "The entrance to this shelter was here, lined up with the corner of the school." He sucked on his toothless gums and stabbed the ground with the toe of his well-worn boot. "To get to the door, you'll have to dig down a fair old way. There's a good few feet of dirt on the roof, and the door was sunk down, see, with steps down on the outside and wooden stairs on the inside. Don't know about digging it up, though. Should leave the past alone."

Miss Pratt looked up from glowering at some mud on her elegant stiletto shoe. "Do you think there would be anything down there, if we did let the children go ahead?"

"Bones of a few dead rats, I suppose. I remember I left my comic book down there. Shouldn't think there's much else. Few old benches, maybe. You should leave the past alone."

"Would you be willing to oversee the children's efforts, Mr. Martin?" Miss Pratt asked. "Mr. Schmidt would be with them at all times to make sure they behave."

"I'll come," Mr. Martin agreed, looking Miss Pratt straight in the eye. He spoke slowly and distinctly, as if he was addressing a particularly dense child. "But know this, Miss, that it's against my better judgment. We are much better leaving the past alone."

❱ ❱ ❱

London clay has to be the worst thing in the world to dig, and we had to shift about a million tons of the stuff. The school had hired a man with a digging machine to start the hole and to shore up the sides with wood, but as we got closer to the door, we had to dig by hand. We worked in relays—two digging and two lugging the soil out of the trench.

I leaned on my spade and wiped my face with a grubby hand. "Are you sure this was such a good idea, Marina? I don't know about finding the door; we'll be in China soon."

"Just think of it as weight-training," Marina puffed, straightening her glasses. "We'll be strong enough to send Quigs into orbit."

She stabbed through the clay with all her might. Clang! We looked at each other in wonder. Could we have reached the door? She drew her spade out and struck again. Even Quigs looked excited as once more, the sound of metal hitting metal rang out.

Mr. Schmidt jumped down into the trench and clawed away the clay with his bare hands. *"Ja, ja!"* he exclaimed in German. "Yes. It feels like a handle. And wait, it is soft and rotten, but yes, it is a door. Ha! We are through to the shelter. We will dig and scrape until we have exposed the whole door and then on Saturday, we will open it properly—with the ceremony befitting finding such an artifact. We will dress in the nineteen-forties clothing we used for our class play last week, *ja*, and we will take pictures inside the shelter. Do you remember the old Leica camera I used to take pictures of the play? Well, it dates from the war, so even that will be authentic."

Mr. Martin's sharp blue eyes peered down at us from the rim of the trench. He shook his head and sighed. "You should leave the past alone."

〉〉〉

If I'd known then what I know now . . .

CHAPTER 2

⟫⟫⟫ Saturday, June 8, 2002

M r. Schmidt, Quigs, Marina, and I anxiously awaited Mr. Martin. I wasn't surprised Miss Pratt hadn't come. She'd probably realized how filthy the shelter would be and had thought better of it.

Quigs always enjoyed a good whine, and today was no exception. "Come on, sir. Can't we get this over and done with? I feel like a complete idiot in this getup. My knees are cold in these rotten shorts and this sweater itches."

"No, we will wait. But look what I have for you here. I have made exact replicas of ration books and identity cards for you, each with your name on the front, and look, I have even made you gas masks. They don't work, but they will look good in the pictures."

"What about you, sir? Do you have a ration book?" I asked.

"Why certainly. Here we are—Henry Smith."

"That's not your name."

"Ha! What chance would Heinrich Schmidt have had living in London in the war? So, Henry Smith I would be."

Mr. Martin pedaled up on his ancient black bicycle and leaned it carefully against the school wall. His eyes looked strange. A gray cloud veiled their usual pale blue iciness.

"Leave the past alone, I said, but no. You wouldn't listen. Well, you've found the perishing shelter, so let's get on with it, if the door will even open. Been shut for over half a century."

The hinges groaned and screamed in protest as Mr. Schmidt slowly wrenched the door open. At last, the door gave up the struggle and we gazed down into the gaping chasm of the shelter. I leaned forward and peered into the darkness as Mr. Schmidt flashed his torch around.

"The stairs are still here." He tested one gently with his foot. "They appear to be sound. Who shall go first?"

Quigs forgot to be bored. His eyes shone eagerly. He leaped down the stairs two at a time, with Marina and me close behind him. The air smelled damp and stale, sort of mushroomy. The thought of slugs and slowworms slithered through my mind. I had to force myself not to charge back up the moldy, slime-covered stairs to the comfort of the June sunshine.

"Wouldn't listen. Told you to leave the past alone," Mr. Martin's querulous voice wafted down.

I reached up to help him down the stairs. A shiver ran through me as he placed his clammy hand in mine and crept slowly downwards.

"Come on, Mr. Schmidt," I called, trying to shake off my unease.

The top stair cracked ominously under Mr. Schmidt's weight. As he made a desperate grab at the shaky handrail, the rotten timbers gave in to the ravages of time and, with a sickening thud, he tumbled to the floor below. The rusty hinges scraped a final grating rasp as the door slammed shut, plunging us into darkness.

When the class had visited Chislehurst Caves, the guide had told us that few people in the modern world ever experience true darkness. With a bubble of hysteria rising inside me, I realized we might be the exceptions. The suffocating blackness hurt my eyes as they strained against it.

"Sir?" I quavered.

No reply.

Marina whispered, "Sophie, do you think he's dead?" Then louder, "Mr. Schmidt? Mr. Martin?"

No reply.

"Mr. Schmidt? Mr. Martin?" we shouted, together.

Still no reply.

"Old Martin's probably died from shock." Quigs actually sounded frightened.

Marina recovered first. "Where's the torch? Mr. Schmidt must have dropped it. It must be here somewhere."

We crawled around with our hands outstretched, searching. I screamed as something grabbed my ankle.

"Only me, silly." Quigs' voice sounded loud in the darkness. "Ah ha! Found it. Wonder if it still works?"

Our relief as the beam of light cut through the thick gloom quickly turned to horror as we saw the crimson-stained chunk of concrete beside Mr. Schmidt's head.

"First aid," I whispered, "Think! A.B.C.." Marina and Quigs stared at me. I repeated it louder. "A.B.C. Airway, breathing, circulation."

I put my face close to Mr. Schmidt's mouth. Yes. He was breathing. My hands shook and I struggled to keep my voice steady as the hysteria bubble threatened to engulf me.

"Recovery position. Turn him on his side to help him breathe better. Unless he's broken his neck. Oh, Marina, you don't think he's broken his neck, do you?"

Marina simply stared at me mutely, her fist pressed against her mouth.

I forced myself to concentrate. "When I took first aid, they taught us how to make a neck collar out of a newspaper."

Quigs flashed the light around the floor. He swooped down on a newspaper that decades ago someone had left lying on a bench. It was disgustingly damp and dirty, but it was all we had. I folded it into thirds. Quigs peeled off his sweater and held it out to me.

"Here, Soph, use this to tie it on."

I nodded and carefully secured the makeshift collar. "Help me to move him. I'll hold his head straight and you two roll him onto his side. Okay. Now, circulation. Stop the bleeding. Heads bleed a lot. What can we use for a bandage?"

Quigs' eyes widened as Marina quickly stepped out of her slip.

"No comments, Quigs," she warned, glaring at him. "Not one."

"Here, give me that." Quigs produced a penknife from his pocket and swiftly tore the cotton fabric into strips, which I wound around Mr. Schmidt's head. That would have to do until we got out. If we got out.

With a jolt, I remembered Mr. Martin. I grabbed the torch from

Quigs and shone it around the shelter. He wasn't there. Mr. Martin had gone. Disappeared. Vanished. I zigzagged the light around the shelter again—across the floor, up and down the walls, and nonsensically, over the ceiling.

"Are you looking for Mr. Martin?" Marina asked. "Maybe he knows another way out. Here, give me that."

She shone the torchlight methodically around the shelter, searching the walls inch by inch for another exit. She shook her head. "Well, who knows where he's gone? Our problem is, how do *we* get out?" She flashed the sliver of light on the shattered remains of the stairs and then up to the door.

Mr. Schmidt groaned softly and struggled to sit up, groping at the bandage and the collar. "What happened? What is this?"

"You fell through the stairs, sir, and we didn't know if your neck was broken, so Sophie made you a collar to hold it still and Quigs' sweater is holding it on. Holding the collar on, that is, not your neck. Oh, sir, your neck's not broken, is it?" Marina's words tumbled out.

Mr. Schmidt gingerly moved his head from side to side. "I don't believe so, Marina. Sophie, would you mind if I took this collar off? I can see why Quigs grumbled about the sweater being itchy. And how is everyone else? I hope nobody else was injured and that I was the only one foolish enough to try gymnastics in an air-raid shelter. Where is Mr. Martin?"

Quigs spoke up. "We don't know, sir. We can't figure out where he went. The old coot's probably hiding somewhere and is going to jump out to scare us. Ooooooh! I'm the ghost of bomb shelters past!"

"Shut up, Quigs," Marina and I said in unison. Mr. Schmidt continued, "Right. We'll get out, find some more lights and hunt for Mr. Martin. It would be foolish for me to go up the stairs first; I might destroy them totally this time. So who shall go first?"

I whispered, "I'm the lightest. The stairs might bear my weight."

"Good girl. Quigs and I will stand underneath to catch you if you fall. Marina, light the stairs for her."

Oh, to be caught by Mr. Schmidt! With my luck, though, I'd probably land on his head and knock him out again, or end up being caught by Quigs. Gross.

Marina nodded, and shone the light on the stairs to guide me. I balanced carefully on the remaining fragments of the top stair and pushed the door. No good. Wouldn't budge. With a strength born of fear and fury, I heaved my skinny shoulder against it, once, twice, until on the third try, it burst open. Below me, Marina and Quigs let out a cheer.

The bright sunlight dazzled me after the dusty gloom of the shelter. I closed my eyes briefly and reopened them, grabbing the doorpost for support as the world churned around me. Everything was the same—and yet, different. There was the school, just as before—but different. The window frames were painted brown, not white. Brown tape criss-crossed each pane of glass. High walls of sandbags guarded the entrance to the shelter. In the distance, a line of silvery blimps floated in the sky, bouncing on their tethers. Barrage balloons?

"Sophie?" Marina called from below. "Sophie, are you okay?"

My voice came out as a thin croak from my dry throat. "I'm okay, Marina. But . . . the world isn't. I . . . I . . . something's happened. I don't know what, but something's happened." I stepped outside as Marina and Quigs ran up the stairs.

"It's a joke. Someone's playing a prank. It's a good one, too," Quigs laughed.

Marina scowled at him. "Don't be silly. Who could do this? Who'd paint the school, just as a joke? Pile those sandbags there? Change everything?" Her voice faltered. My hand found hers and we clung to each other. "What's going on, Sophie?"

We stood silently, trying to make sense of the scene around us, gazing up as engines droned overhead. Spitfires. I'd seen them before when I'd visited the Biggin Hill air show with my father. Spitfires were supposed to be at the Biggin Hill air show; they were not supposed to be flying over Penge in South London.

Mr. Schmidt came up behind us. "My goodness, what has happened here? My head . . . maybe I banged my head worse than I thought. Maybe I am dreaming."

"What, all four of us dreaming the same thing?" Quigs scoffed. "This is so cool. We've gone back to the war. The bomb shelter must have been a time portal or something, and it's taken us back to the war."

"But that only happens on television and in movies. It can't really happen," I said, uncertainly.

"Well, you come up with another explanation then. Look around you, stupid! What other explanation could there possibly be?"

Mr. Schmidt's voice was filled with wonder. "Although I hate to admit it, Quigs must be right. We can't understand everything in the universe. Things that would have seemed impossible centuries ago, we now take for granted—like television, for instance. Who would have thought a thousand years ago that pictures and sound could travel through the air into a box in someone's home?"

We left the entrance between the sandbags and looked around. The tall iron railings that should separate the school from the pavement were gone. The few cars on the street looked like they'd driven straight out of an old movie. People in drab clothes hurried along, keeping a wary eye on the sky as the throb of aircraft engines became more and more persistent.

"We had better find out exactly what the date is. What clues are there?" Mr. Schmidt said.

"Don't need clues," Quigs replied. "I know the date."

We stared at him.

"Blimey, I'm not as stupid as you lot think. When I handed you the paper for Mr. Schmidt's neck, Sophie, I looked at the date. September 12, 1940, it said. So it must be around then."

Mr. Schmidt smiled. "Well done, Quigs. I always suspected you came complete with brain. We must sort out a plan of action. We can't just stand here; people will start to wonder about us and we must not arouse suspicion. And we will need our identity cards, ration books and gas masks."

"They don't work, sir."

"That doesn't matter. Gas was never actually used. But we'll need them for show. Ah! And my old Leica camera is still down in the shelter. But no, maybe it is better if we hide the camera or destroy it altogether. It is German. I am German. I used that camera when we did our play about what could have happened if the Germans had invaded England, and I took pictures of the class doing Nazi salutes. Quigs was absent that day with an upset stomach, but you girls were there. What would people think if they found those pictures?"

The horror of the situation dawned on me. Surely no one would suspect us of being Nazis, would they?

"But even after we get rid of the camera, you three must stay away from me, if for no other reason than I have a German accent. You would be endangering your own freedom if they found you with me. I am not sure what the penalty would have been for harboring a German spy."

"But can't we just figure out how to get back home?" I asked. "Why do we even need ration books and gas masks and things? We'll simply go home." Hot tears stung my eyes. "Maybe if we all go down into the shelter again and close the door, then when we open it again, we'll be back in the twenty-first century."

Without waiting for an answer, I ran to the shelter and ground to a halt in amazement. A freshly-painted door and solid stairs replaced the rotting door and crumbling steps. I darted down into the shadows below, the others close behind me. Dense darkness enveloped us as Mr. Schmidt shut the door. Marina flipped on the torch.

"How long do you think we have to stay here before we go back up again? A minute, an hour, a day?" My hysteria bubble exploded, drowning me in a flood of misery.

"I don't know, Sophie," Marina said. "I've never been a time-traveler before. Now, what about Mr. Martin? I wonder where he's gone."

"Reckon he's the key," stated Quigs, firmly. "I think this is all that old buzzard's fault. Remember how he kept rattling on about leaving the past alone? I bet he knew this would happen, and now he's run away, scarpered. Or, more likely, he just vanished."

I had to agree with Quigs. This whole thing was impossible, but I was quickly learning some things are more impossible than others. And if Mr. Martin was the key to getting back to our own time, then we would have a problem. Because first, we'd have to find the young Mr. Martin.

"Well, I'm not going back," Quigs repeated himself, louder. "I'm not going back. I hate my life at home. I hate it! I've been thinking of running away for ages, but I didn't want to be homeless and sleeping in a shop doorway. I'm not going back. I'm staying here. It's not like anyone would even care if they never saw me again."

Marina put her hand on Quigs' arm. "Of course they would care. You have a wonderful life. Look at where you live. Look at all the cool stuff you have. You're always getting new things."

It was true. The Quigleys lived in a huge house with tennis courts and an indoor pool in the best part of Beckenham, the town next to Penge. Quigs had his own television in his bedroom; I didn't even have my own room.

Quigs snatched his arm away. "Things! Yeah, I have lots of things. And parents who are always at work or away on business." He barked a short, harsh laugh. When he continued, his voice was fierce, flint-hard. "But I'd rather they were away than at home because they can't be in the same room for more than five minutes without—without—"

I was horrified to see tears well up in Quigs' eyes.

"He hits her," he whispered. "Until I got to be nearly as tall as him and started to hit him back, he used to hit me, too. Remember how people used to think I was clumsy because of all my bruises?" He broke off and chewed his quivering lips. "But now, he hits only her. And who seems to be the cause of all the fights? Me, that's who. Always me. Without me, they'd be happy again. I know they would. I'd rather live with you—" he stabbed his finger at me, "in your basement flat, even if it does get damp when it rains, or with you—" he pointed viciously at Marina, "in your council house. So you don't have things. Who cares? At least—at least your parents might even care if you were stuck sixty years ago; if—if they even knew we're stuck sixty years ago, they'd care." His angry voice faded into a miserable sniff.

What could I say? All those years of envying Quigs, of wishing I lived in his house in Beckenham instead of in the poky basement flat I shared with my sister and my mother in Penge, and for what? He was right. If Mum knew, if Dad and his new wife, Sylvia, knew we were stuck, they'd care. They'd fight to get me back. They'd find a way through the time portal. They'd even come into the nineteen forties to live with me rather than live in the twenty-first century without me. I knew that. Quigs knew no such thing.

Mr. Schmidt, as usual, knew the right thing to do. He passed Quigs a handkerchief and fixed his attention on us, giving Quigs some privacy to sort himself out.

"Children, we must decide what to do now. If we can't get back to our own time for a while, then we must figure out how to live here. We must concoct a story that sounds plausible."

Mr. Schmidt thought for a minute. "Ah! Got it! Actually, the story is rather sad. You children lived next door to each other in the East End. Your houses got bombed. You are orphans. So sad. I was your teacher and a good friend of your families, so I took you in. And then, what should happen, but my house was bombed too. So there we were. No homes. No money. No clothes. All we owned was on our backs, and with the few shillings in my pocket, I thought I would bring you out for a little journey. We had just got off the train and the air raid started. So here we are. What are the problems?"

This was comfortingly like school. Marina raised her hand. "Money, sir. We don't have any. I know we have fake ration books, but without money, they're not much good, are they?"

"No, they certainly are not. But while we're talking about the ration books, we'd better finish off the front covers. You will note I put your names on them, but fortunately, I didn't have the time to look up your addresses. So we shall write fake addresses on them. As luck would have it, I taught in the East End last year, which was very heavily bombed in the Blitz, and I remember the name of a street that was totally destroyed. So that will be your address. Give me your books." We sat silently while Mr. Schmidt took out his fountain pen and carefully wrote addresses on the covers. "So, now we have some identification, at least. What else do we need?"

"A place to live," I chimed in. "We can't stay in this shelter forever. We'll be discovered sooner or later."

"Yes, that is true. Quigs? Do you have anything to contribute to the discussion?"

Quigs shook his head, sullenly cleaning his fingernails with his penknife.

Mr. Schmidt's voice softened.

"And remember, you are going to have to convince people your parents have just died."

"Good riddance," Quigs muttered.

Tears welled in my eyes. I clutched Marina's hand.

"My parents are dead," she whispered, ending with a gulp. "No, sir, I can't say that."

"You must, Marina. You must. And if it makes you cry to say it, so much the better, because we must not arouse suspicion. People must believe our account. So you have no choice. Until we get out of here, your parents are—dead."

He clapped his hands, a habit he had when calling the class to order, and his tone became brisk once more.

"Well, then, I suggest we make a plan of action. I, for one, am feeling quite hungry. I don't know what the time is, but it must be well past lunch and getting near teatime. I wonder if there is a soup kitchen for poor homeless people around here. Let's go and find out."

Teatime. Mum would be expecting me home soon. Marina's parents would be looking for her, too. As for Quigs? I hoped his parents would stop fighting long enough to wonder where he could be. I bit my lip. Breakfast at home, and at war before tea.

CHAPTER 3

❯❯❯ Sunday, September 15, 1940

At that moment, the loud, undulating wail of an air-raid siren split the air.

Quigs jumped up. "This is more like it! Now we're going to see some action. I'm going outside."

"Sit down. At once! You will do no such thing. Gather up your gas masks. Come here. Sit with me," Mr. Schmidt said, turning off the torch and hastily stuffing the camera in the corner under the bench. At the top of the stairs, a pale shaft of light widened as the door burst open and dozens of people cascaded down into the shelter.

"Move along quickly now. Come along, don't have all day. This isn't a blooming picnic, you know. Come on." A thin man in a steel helmet marked with a large "W" herded people into the shelter as quickly as he could.

An old woman settled down beside me and took out her knitting. "Old bossy boots. Worse than a flaming sheepdog nipping at your heels. Wish he'd hurry up and light the lamps. I'm trying to do a cable pattern. Can't flaming do it in the dark, can I? What's the point of making us stagger around in the dark until the door's closed when it's daylight outside? That's what I want to know." She mumbled away cantankerously, jabbing at her knitting with the needles.

The low moan of aircraft engines hummed along to the tune of the siren's howl. Occasional bursts of gunfire—I supposed from anti-aircraft guns—kept rhythm.

"Get a flaming move on!" The air-raid warden shouted from the door.

"Come on, Mr. Schmidt—I mean Smith, I must see what's going on. Think what a good mark I could get on my project if I gave an eyewitness account of a dogfight," Quigs pleaded, tugging on Mr. Schmidt's sleeve.

"You won't have a project if you are dead, young man. Now sit down before I get really angry."

A pretty, blonde woman with a flame-haired boy of about four squeezed in beside Quigs. "Room for a small one? Bit cozy down here, isn't it? What are your names?" The questions came like machine-gun fire, without pauses for answers. "My name is Esther Quigley, and this is my son, Joseph. My husband's in the RAF, somewhere in Kent. Huh! At least, I hope he's somewhere in Kent. Not somewhere over Germany. Still, from the sound of that out there, I don't suppose he's any safer in Kent."

Well! Esther Quigley. What were the odds of that happening? I glanced across at Quigs, who sat with his mouth agape. When we'd started the history unit on World War II, Quigs told the class his great-grandfather had flown Spitfires in the war. So Esther must be Quigs' great-grandma, which would make the little boy Quigs' grandpa. A giggle rose in me at this ludicrous concept, until I remembered that Quigs' great-grandfather had been shot down and killed over the Channel. Suddenly the situation wasn't funny anymore.

Marina whispered in my ear, "Quigs said his great-granddad died on September 27, 1940. I remember the date because it was exactly fifty years before my parents got married. We know it's at least September twelfth today, but I wonder exactly what the date is."

The man sitting across the narrow aisle from us turned the page of his newspaper. Marina and I leaned forward and strained to see the date. September 15, 1940. Quigs' great-granddad would die in less than two weeks. I looked across at pretty Esther Quigley, bouncing Joseph on her knee. This woman's husband—this little boy's daddy—was going to die. We knew it. They didn't. And there was nothing we could do about it.

❱ ❱ ❱

At first, the rumbling was almost soothing and familiar—a bit like an underground train coming into the station. Then came the first boom—muffled and distant. Someone started to count. One . . . two . . . three. Boom! Closer that time. One . . . two . . . three. Boom! Closer still. I took up the counting in my head. Boom! The crashes of a thousand giants playing kick-the-can with an oil drum reverberated through the shelter. Another count. This time, I heard a shrill whistle as the bomb fell. "Wait for it," Esther said, drawing Joseph closer, burying her face in his hair. The giants shook the earth again. Dust rained down from the ceiling as the dim electric lamps swung wildly. Surely the next one couldn't be any nearer. I clutched Marina's hand tightly and screwed my eyes shut. Punctuated by loud bursts of gunfire, the deafening scream of the bomb hurtling earthward grabbed and squeezed me until I couldn't breathe. It was a relief when the gut-wrenching explosion ended the ghastly shriek.

A scream. A prayer. A baby's cry. A glass bottle shattering on the floor. Every tiny sound stood out in sharp relief. Everything seemed to be going in slow motion. This was a dream. A nightmare. A nightmare in which Quigs, Marina, Mr. Schmidt, and I did not belong. We shouldn't be here.

Esther's bright voice broke the spell. "Well, always good to hear the explosion. Proves you're alive. Still, some poor beggar probably isn't. I wonder who bought it that time. The electric company in Beckenham got hit at lunchtime. Was hardly worth getting out of the shelter, only to come back again. Jump down, Joseph. Go and see Harry over there. Whew! Blimey, that kid's getting heavy. Got another one on the way, too."

Marina and I exchanged glances. Tears welled up behind Marina's glasses.

"So, where d'you live then? Reckon your street's okay?"

Well, that was a loaded question. It should have been so simple to answer, but I could imagine the response if I'd told her. "Where do you live? Oh, I know where that is. What number? I'll drop by and see you some time."

I was glad when Quigs answered the question as he's a much better liar than I am, having had tons of practice. He told Esther the story Mr. Schmidt had outlined to us earlier, embellishing it with blood and gore and scattered body parts.

With an award-winning acting performance, Quigs sniffed to Esther and said in a choked voice, "Reckon you must be a relative. My last name is Quigley, and I don't think there are many of us around."

"Well, fancy that. You certainly have the Quigley red hair, that's for sure. I didn't know there were any Quigleys in the East End."

"Well, there are. Here's my identification card, see. Nathan Quigley, that's me. Though everyone calls me Quigs. And that's Marina Curtis, and Sophie Pinkerton—they're all right, for girls—and Mr. Sch—Mr. Smith." He caught himself in the nick of time.

"Well, pleased to make your acquaintance, I'm sure. Did you know you had relatives in Beckenham? Is that why you came here?"

"Well, my dad had mentioned some sort of relative living here. We thought you must be ever so posh to live in Beckenham. My dad wasn't posh." Quigs broke off, gave a little sob and sniffed loudly, wiping his nose on his hand. Esther dug around in her handbag and gave him a hankie.

"There, there, never mind. Poor kid. Horrible old war. Here, are you hungry? Never met a Quigley man who wasn't. When the siren went, I was on my way back from visiting my sister and she gave me some biscuits. Here, have one. Your friends, too. So, what are you going to do now that you have nowhere to live? Do you have a place to stay?"

"No. I don't know what we'll do. Maybe we can sleep down here."

"You can't live in an air-raid shelter. Don't be daft. No, you come home with me, at least for a while. You're family, and families stick together. Especially in a war."

Quigs stared at her.

"But what about Mr. Smith and the girls?"

"Them too, of course. Blimey, I think if this war carries on like this, we'll all be living in one another's houses. Wish that all clear would blow. If I don't use the toilet soon, I think I'll burst. I'm not using one of those buckets behind the screen over there."

As if on cue, the steady tone of the "all clear" siren sounded. People gathered up their belongings and their children, and made their way to the stairs.

Nothing could have prepared us for the horror awaiting us outside the shelter. Hungry tongues of fire lapped at the gutted remains of shops and houses, which belched dense clouds of dust and smoke as they groaned and crashed in smoldering heaps. The air—if you could call it that—was a thick, grimy soup, heavy with the acrid stench of oil and, strangely, fireworks. Bells ringing urgently, fire engines and ambulances jostled their way past people standing hypnotized as they watched the flames devour their world.

"Come on, this way. I'm only over the road." Holding Joseph tightly in her arms, Esther hurried us across the road and up the neat path to a handsome Victorian house.

Quigs pinched my arm, whispering, "My grandparents still live in this house. Joseph must have lived here all his life. How cool is that?"

Esther heaved a sigh of relief as she opened the front door and put Joseph down. "The sitting room's through there. I'm just going to run upstairs. Won't be long." She looked at Mr. Schmidt. "When I come down, I'll do a better bandaging job on your head."

The sitting room was a snug oasis from the awful outside. I could imagine Esther huddled up next to the huge, old-fashioned radio as she listened to the BBC and wondered where her husband was. I walked over to Quigs, who was running his fingers along the edge of a tall, glass-fronted cabinet.

"In sixty years time, a clay pot I made in school will be in there," he said softly in my ear. "Gran and Granddad always put the things I gave them on display. Mum and Dad never even looked at them." I gave his arm a quick squeeze as a shadow crossed his face, but then he stepped back, embarrassed. For more than six years, I had considered Quigs to be the lowest of the low. After less than six hours in 1940, I was starting to wonder if I'd been wrong.

Quigs wandered over to the mantel and studied a photo of a man in a Royal Air Force uniform. The man could have been Quigs in twenty years time, the resemblance was so striking.

"That's Fred, my husband," Esther said from the doorway. "Blimey, don't you look like him? No doubt about it, you're a Quigley all right. And if you're like him in character, you won't go far wrong. Hope he comes home on leave soon; I can't wait to see you two together. Come on into the kitchen. It's warmest in there. I know it's not cold outside, but I feel a bit chilly."

We followed her down the passage into the kitchen. Despite her sunny voice and smile, her hands shook as she filled the kettle and lit the gas stove.

"I'll be glad of your company actually. Bit lonely in this big old house with only Joseph. My mother was going to stay with me while my husband's away, but she's gone to visit my aunt in the country for a while. I don't blame her. I'd send Joseph down to them, but I couldn't bear to be without him. It's bad enough being without Fred. Oh, I miss him. He doesn't know he's going to be a dad again. I'm waiting till he comes home on leave to tell him."

Marina shot me a stricken glance and said, "Why don't you write and tell him?"

"No, I want to surprise him and tell him in person. Hope it's not too long before he comes, or I'll be the size of a barrage balloon." Her veneer was starting to crack and she blinked hard. "Never mind. Plenty worse off than us." Esther carried a bowl of water over to Mr. Schmidt and started to unwind the makeshift bandage from his head, chatting on as she cleaned his wound. "Now then, better think about sleeping arrangements. The girls can have the room with a big double bed. You don't mind sharing, do you? Quigs, I'll put a camp bed in Joseph's room for you, if that's all right. And Mr. Smith, there's a single bed in the spare room. It's a bit small, I'm afraid."

For the first time, Mr. Schmidt spoke. "Mrs. Quigley, you are being so kind, I don't know what to say. But we have no money to pay you. No money even for our food. We cannot impose."

She stopped dabbing at his head and looked at him sharply. "Are—are you German? Not that it matters," she continued hastily. "I dare say there's good Germans as well as bad Englishmen,— but—*are* you? If I'm not being nosy."

You could have heard a pin drop. I held my breath. Even Joseph stared at Mr. Schmidt.

"I am from Switzerland, Mrs. Quigley. My parents were English and went to Switzerland to teach before I was born. Three years ago, I came to England to teach. Don't be alarmed about the accent;

the Swiss accent is very like the German to the untrained ear. But yes, you are right. There are good and bad people in every country."

I let my breath out slowly. I had no idea Mr. Schmidt was such a good liar.

Esther dried his head and applied a clean bandage. "Well, that's all right then, isn't it? You're not to worry about money just now. I have a bit put aside for emergencies. And if you're a teacher, I'm sure they'll be glad to have you across the road. Most of their teachers have joined up. When you're earning, you can pay me back."

I'd never met anyone who could talk nonstop like Esther. But at least while she chattered away, Marina and I didn't have to say those horrible words "My parents are dead." I looked around the kitchen, which was very like my Nan's. Brown linoleum, wearing out in places, covered the floor. There was no fridge, but through a half-open door, I could see a pantry with a marble counter. The gas stove stood in the alcove where the fireplace would have been when the house had been built in the last century—that is to say, Esther's last century, not mine. Everything seemed surprisingly normal. I became dimly aware of someone calling my name.

"Sophie! Oh, for crying out loud. That girl lives in a world of her own."

"Oh, sorry Mr. Schm—Smith. Were you speaking to me?"

"Mrs. Quigley, er, Esther, asked if bubble and squeak is okay for your tea. Can you answer the lady, please?"

"Oh! Yes, thank you very much, that would be lovely. Is there anything I can do to help? I always helped my mum at home." My trembling voice trailed off miserably. Oh, how I wished I was at home with my mother and my sister, Erica.

"Thanks. It'll be good for you to keep busy. Here are some boiled potatoes; if you can slice them for me, that would be good. And Marina, can you wash the cabbage? Watch out for bugs. Been quite a summer for them."

Quigs snickered as Marina shuddered.

"And you, young Master Quigs, can stop your sniggering. You can take the cabbage trimmings and give them to the rabbits."

"Ah, rabbits!" Marina and I chorused.

"Yes, rabbits. And don't go getting fond of them, either. Because they're dinner."

I gagged.

"You don't kill them yourself, do you?" Marina asked, incredulously.

"No, don't be daft. The caretaker over at the school does it for me. Comes and gets one, does the necessary, and gives it back all nice and clean. He keeps the skin. Makes gloves and things and sells them. You'll get on well with his son, Quigs. You must be the same age. Twelvish?" Quigs nodded. "Well, he'll be a friend for you, then. Herbert Martin's his name."

I looked over at Mr. Schmidt, who raised an eyebrow and shrugged. I supposed "Martin" was a common enough surname, but I wondered if this was our Mr. Martin. And if he was, how on earth would we know?

❯ ❯ ❯

Mr. Schmidt, Quigs, Marina, and I huddled close together in the sitting room, talking quietly while Esther put Joseph to bed. "Not that it's really worth it," she had said. "We'll be up again in a few hours and into the Anderson shelter."

"You children had better call me Henry," Mr. Schmidt suggested. "You've all nearly slipped and called me Mr. Schmidt instead of Mr. Smith, so it would be much easier if you called me Henry, instead. But," he glowered at us, "if any of you dares to call me Henry when we get back to the twenty-first century, you'll have detention for a week."

"Do you think we'll get back . . . Henry?" My heart fluttered at being able to call Mr. Schmidt by his first name. Oh! If the other girls could see me now, sitting on the sofa with Henry, drinking tea, and calling him by his first name. Well, a version of his first name, anyway. I yanked myself back to reality just in time to hear the end of his answer.

"Well, if we got here, we can get back again. I'm sure time portals work in both directions."

"Know a lot about time portals, do you, Hank?" Quigs sneered.

"Quigs, Henry is one thing. I draw the line at Hank. Mind your manners and cut the sarcasm, or I'll give you five hundred lines to write, right now. That should keep you busy until we get back to our time, even if we have to go the slow way. No, I do not know a lot about time portals. But it would make sense, as much as any of this makes sense. Now, if the Martins at the school are the same family as our Mr. Martin comes from, then maybe one of them will be the key to getting us back to our own time. If Herbert is twelve in 1940, then in our time, he will be in his seventies, which would be the right age. Oh, speaking about age. Don't forget you are all born in 1928 or '29. You'll have to give your birthdates when you register for school."

I ventured, "Sir, would it be wise to go to school? We might change history if we are in contact with too many people."

"Ha! You'd change history if you managed to stay awake for a whole day," Quigs retorted quickly. He grimaced as I aimed a sharp kick at his shin.

"You will go to school until we devise a method of getting out of here. I suppose since it's now September, you're all three months older than you were in our time and not nine months younger. And remember, your class in 1940 was called First Form. Year Eight is Second Form, and so on. We'll get you registered tomorrow. Maybe Esther can help."

"Maybe Esther can help what?" Esther breezed into the room and tossed herself into a soft armchair. "Joseph didn't want to go to sleep. He's afraid there's going to be another raid. Probably will be. That reminds me. The Anderson shelter is in the back garden about five yards from the house. It only has four bunks and there are six of us, so it'll be a bit tight. I hope the war is over before winter. It's not too bad this time of year, but it'll be freezing in there in January. Anyway, you were saying you needed my help with something?"

"Yes, if we are going to stay here for awhile, I think the children should be registered for school as soon as possible. I believe you said the school over the road is a boys' school?"

"That's right. There's a girls' school not far from here. I'll be delighted to help register them. Oh! Clothes! They'll have a school uniform, of course, but they can't spend the rest of their time in what they have. And, Henry, if you don't mind me saying so, neither can you. You're about the same size as my husband. I know he won't mind if you borrow some of his things. The girls can wear some of my sweaters, and we can shorten some old skirts. The boy next door is a bit bigger than Quigs; I'll run over in the morning and see if he can spare some old clothes. There! That's settled."

The mantel clock struck ten. Esther stood up. "We'd better go to bed. Don't know when the Jerries will be back. Get some sleep now, before we have to go to the shelter. Come on, I'll show you to your rooms." She chattered on as we turned out the lamps and followed her up the stairs. I wondered about Mum and Erica, and Dad and Sylvia. What were they thinking? They must be out of their minds with worry. Or maybe "real" time had stopped. I hoped so, sighing.

"Don't worry," Marina whispered. "We'll get back."

"We won't," Quigs said under his breath. "We won't get back, because I'm not going back. And that's that!"

CHAPTER 4

⟫⟫⟫ Monday, September 16, 1940

"**S**ophie! Wake up. Sophie!"

Marina pulled the covers from over my head and shook me violently. The wail of the air-raid siren ripped through my sleep-befuddled brain.

"I—what do we do?" I mumbled.

"Put your shoes on, silly. Quick! Oh, hurry up."

The drone of aircraft engines grew louder as I hopped to the door, one shoe on and one shoe off.

On the landing, Mr. Schmidt swung into bossy schoolteacher mode. "Hurry up, girls. Move, Quigs! Esther, give me Joseph."

Esther handed the sleeping child to Mr. Schmidt and led the way down the stairs. She picked up a torch from the kitchen table and turned off the overhead light, plunging the house into darkness. Esther directed the narrow beam of light down to the ground.

"Okay, careful. Quigs, shut the door behind you."

From every direction, swarms of fighter planes buzzed angrily. Antiaircraft gunfire rattled in the distance. Flames danced along the horizon. Searchlights criss-crossed the sky, casting circles of light where they met the clouds. I had never been particularly brave in a thunderstorm, and this was far, far worse. At least a thunderstorm was not consciously trying to kill people.

The moonlight's ghostly glow silhouetted the rounded hump of the Anderson shelter, which was buried about three feet into the ground with its top covered with soil. We went down three steps, and ducked through the low doorway.

"Come on. Hurry up," Esther urged us along. "Here, Henry, put Joseph down on that bunk. That kid could sleep through anything. Wish he could sleep through this entire rotten war and wake up when it's all over."

The interior of the Anderson shelter was a bit like a large tin can, about four and a half feet wide and about seven feet long. The curved roof must have been about six feet high in the middle; I noticed Mr. Schmidt's head just touched it when he stood up straight. There were two very narrow bunk beds on either side, with a little cabinet at one end, and even a bookcase which held a selection of books and games. Two old kitchen chairs stood against one wall. The air was stale and earthy, like my grandfather's garden shed.

Esther fished around in a square biscuit tin, produced a box of matches and lit the hurricane lamps. "There! That's better. Quite cozy by candlelight." Her brave smile wavered slightly as the sound of distant aerial fighting grew closer. "Been spending more time in here lately than I'd planned. Blimey! When Fred put this thing up, I wasn't planning to spend *any* time in it. Have to see if I can get a couple more comfy chairs, and maybe a bit of carpet. We're lucky; Fred's ever so handy and this shelter is much more watertight than some peoples' are. Mr. Barnes' shelter down the road leaked like a vegetable strainer until Fred looked at it. Dryer outside than it was in. And at least ours has a real door. Most people only have a bit of canvas in the doorway. Fred had the novel idea of hinging the top bunks, so they can be hooked out of the way—see? I don't think anyone else has thought of that. So, all in all, this is Beckenham Palace."

Every banging, crashing, screaming bomb echoed around our tin can. I sat on the edge of Joseph's bunk and plugged my ears against the dreadful din.

"Sir, *please* can I go outside and watch?" Quigs begged. "Oh, sir, please?"

"Quigs, sit down and shut up. If I hear one more word about going outside, I shall give you detention for the rest of your life. Which if you did leave the shelter, might not be too long." Mr. Schmidt smiled grimly.

"Right, Quigs, do you fancy a game of gin rummy?" Esther pulled a pack of playing cards out of the bookcase. "Anyone else?"

"I'm in!" Marina chirped.

"Sophie?"

I shook my head, my fingers shoved tight in my ears.

Mr. Schmidt rubbed his hands together gleefully. "Deal me in. And be prepared to lose."

I looked at the clock on the cabinet. Half past twelve. I wondered what Mum was doing. Bet she wasn't asleep. I wondered if the police were at my house, taking statements or whatever they did when someone vanished off the face of the earth. Oh, Mum, Mum—

To my horror, I gave a noisy sob. In an instant, Esther was beside me, her arm around my shoulder.

"Oh, Sophie, sweetie, don't worry, you'll be all right. I know it's hideous, and you're thinking about your family. It's difficult, but you mustn't think; not too hard, anyway. Remember your family always, but you have to look after yourself now. Always look forward, never back—that's what my grandmother used to say. Make your mother proud of you."

Well, that really opened the floodgates. I was vaguely aware of Marina and Quigs staring at me, and of Mr. Schmidt studiously looking the other way. I must get a grip on myself. What a situation—my parents hadn't been born yet, but Esther thought they were dead; Esther's husband was soon to die, and she had no idea. Would life ever be normal again?

❱ ❱ ❱

It was after three in the morning when we crept back into the house, picking our way through the debris. I lay awake for ages after I finally crawled back into bed. At some point during those sleepless hours, I resolved that if I was stuck in this war, I'd better stiffen my upper lip and get on with life—the same as everyone else had to do.

After an all too short and fitful sleep, I awoke to the smell of toast and tea.

"Good morning!" Esther greeted me. "Thought I'd let you have a little lie-in after last night's activities. Marina's a real early bird, isn't she? She was up before me."

I sat up with a start. "Oh! Sorry, did I oversleep? What time is it?"

"Nine o'clock, but don't bother about that. Quigs is still dead to the world. I tried to wake him, but in true Quigley fashion, he just mumbled something and rolled over. Henry has gone off to the school to apply for a teaching job. He cleans up quite nicely, doesn't he? I lent him one of Fred's suits. Good thing they're about the same size, though Henry is a tiny bit taller. Here, move over. I brought an extra cup for myself." Esther put the tray on the bedside table and sat on the bed beside me. She poured two cups of tea and handed me one. "I thought I'd say this in case you were embarrassed about last night. Never feel ashamed of your feelings. You're allowed to cry. If you don't, well, I reckon you'd go mad. If you ever need anyone to talk to about anything at all, just think of me as a big sister. All right?" I nodded. "Good!" She gave me a quick hug, nearly spilling my tea. "Oh, I'm glad you're here. At times when I was all alone with Joseph in that shelter at night, I thought I'd go crazy. It's good to have company. Eat your breakfast and come downstairs. I've found some skirts and things we can alter for you and Marina. It'll be fun."

She whirled out of the room. Toast in hand, I crawled out of bed and opened the heavy blackout curtains. My bedroom overlooked the back garden and the railway line. A London-bound steam engine puffed by, belching black smoke. At the school on the other side of the tracks, a class of six-year-olds was out in the playground exercising while their teacher spent a lot of time blowing her whistle and bellowing. I grinned. Strange how some things don't change in sixty years. Esther's garden was neatly laid out in rows of all types of vegetables; they were even planted on the soil on top of the air-raid shelter. A few rosebushes and shrubs remained, incongruously dotted between the peas and carrots. The rabbit hutch stood against the fence at the back of the garden. I was glad it wasn't right up by the house; the less I saw of the rabbits, the better, if I was expected to eat them.

I hastily got dressed and stuffed the nightgown Esther had lent me into a dresser drawer. I dragged a comb through my hair, made a face in the mirror, and picked up the tea tray.

Crossing the landing, I crashed into Quigs coming out of his bedroom. He groaned. "Blimey, I'd forgotten I'd have to see you and Marina before breakfast. Yuck. Oh well, I guess it's like eating a frog first thing in the morning—nothing worse can happen to you for the rest of the day."

"Likewise, I'm sure," I retorted and flounced downstairs.

Marina was alone in the kitchen, busy sweeping the floor. "Hello, sleepyhead," she greeted me. "Isn't it a lovely day? I simply adore autumn. Though it's a shame we got cheated out of an entire summer, or do you think it will still be June when we get back?"

Mr. Schmidt's voice boomed from the front hall.

"Esther! Children! Wonderful news!"

"What? Hitler's fallen down a mineshaft?" Esther joked, running down the stairs.

"No, silly. Not that wonderful, but wonderful enough. It would seem that two language teachers have left the school recently. Just disappeared. Possibly they were interned; I don't know. But, thanks to that, I am now in the employ of the boys' secondary school, as a languages teacher, and—" he grinned as Quigs came down the stairs, "First Form Master. So, young Quigs, since you are in the First Form, you will still be in my class."

"Fate worse than death!" Quigs quipped.

"And here is the really good part. I explained our circumstances to the Headmaster and told him how kind Mrs. Quigley was to take us in, and he has given me an advance on my pay. So, Esther, I will now be able to pay for our food and lodging. He even said they should be able to sort out an old school blazer for Quigs. Now the sad part, Quigs, is that due to the shortage of air-raid shelter space, the boys only go to school every other week."

Quigs let out a whoop.

"However, you will be given large amounts of homework, which you will do, and not all on the Sunday night before you go back. The Headmaster also phoned Miss Stanley, the Headmistress of the girls' school, and arranged for the girls to be admitted there. So! See what I have accomplished before you lazy bunch were even out of your beds?"

"Hey! I've been up since seven," Marina protested. "I was up before you."

Mr. Schmidt smiled broadly. "So Esther, shall you put on your hat and shall we go shopping? I don't want to wear your husband's clothes all the time."

"I can't go like this, in my old housedress with no makeup on and my hair a mess," Esther said. "You'll have to give me an hour or so."

Once Esther was safely upstairs, Marina asked, "Sir, when you said that some other teachers were interned, what did you mean?"

"Ah! That is what would happen to me if someone found out I was German. Enemy aliens, as German people living in England were called, were sent to places like the Isle of Man during the war. Even English women married to Germans were sent away, because they might be a security risk."

"You mean send messages to the Germans or something?"

"That's right. Their political leanings meant nothing. All that mattered was where they were born. However, after the war, it turned out that some people who disappeared were actually helping the government with intelligence. Enough of that; we have work to do." He pulled out a handful of money from his pocket. "Right, you lot. When the Headmaster gave me a pocketful of change this morning, little did he realize he had also written your morning's lesson plan." We groaned. He glared at us. "You'll remember that we were discussing pounds, shillings and pence in school? Well, you had better be familiar with them. And Quigs, your twelve times table had better improve a bit, because how many pennies were in a shilling?"

"Twelve," Quigs replied in a bored voice. "And twenty shillings in a pound. I know, I know."

"Right. Suppose I give you a shilling, and the item I am buying is eight pence ha'penny, pick out the change you would give me back."

We stared down at the unfamiliar coins, and as usual, Marina was the first one to get the correct answer. Mr. Schmidt drilled us on shillings and "florins" and "ten bob" notes until we heard the bathroom door open upstairs.

Mr. Schmidt stuffed the money back in his pocket. "This will also be the acid test for the ration books. After all, they are forgeries. Very good ones, if I say so myself, but forgeries nevertheless."

"But they aren't actually money," I reasoned. "So it's not like we're stealing, is it?"

"I'm not sure they would look at it that way. There were laws against ration book fraud, you know. And we don't want to give anyone reason to examine anything we do, as we have no identity. I, for one, would be considered a spy; maybe you, too, even though you speak like everyone else and are only children. Hysteria runs high in wartime."

Hysteria was running high in me, too. I swallowed nervously. All of a sudden, this shopping trip was assuming nightmare proportions.

Esther breezed into the kitchen with Joseph in tow. "Well, you're all looking very somber! Shall we walk into Penge or take the bus into Beckenham? Let's make it Beckenham. Quigs, I got some clothes for you from a neighbor. I've put them on your bed, so hurry up and get dressed. Right, then," she continued as Quigs ran up the stairs, "if everyone can give me their ration books, I'll buy some groceries."

I held my breath as Mr. Schmidt handed them to her.

Esther flipped through them. "Oh! All brand-new, I see."

"We had to get new ones because our old ones were lost in the bombing," Mr. Schmidt explained.

"Yes, I expect they were."

I have never been so grateful in my life to see Quigs as I was when he burst into the kitchen, putting an end to this awkward conversation. Esther popped the ration books into her handbag.

"I'll buy the food in Penge later on. Well, come on, then."

Several of the neighbors stood in their front gardens gossiping as we left the house. They stared at us curiously. My cheeks burned as I saw curtains twitch in one house after another.

Esther was obviously conscious of it, too. "Nosy blooming parkers," she muttered. "Got nothing better to do than stand and stare at other people."

"Good morning, Mrs. Jones!" she sang out to an older woman in a thick hairnet and flowery pinafore who was openly gaping at us. "This is the worst one," Esther whispered to us. "If I tell her about you, it will be all around Penge and Beckenham by dinnertime. A regular town crier."

Esther strode over to Mrs. Jones. We followed—what else could we do?

"Good morning, Mrs. Jones," she repeated. "I should like you to meet my houseguests. This is my—nephew, Nathan Quigley, and my friends Mr. Henry Smith, Marina Curtis and Sophie Pinkerton, who'll be staying with me for a while. Mr. Smith will be teaching languages at the boys' school. Goodbye, Mrs. Jones."

Mrs. Jones' jaw dropped farther and farther during Esther's speech. She snapped it closed. "Well, good morning to you, I'm sure. I dare say I shall be seeing you later."

"I dare say. Say goodbye, children. We must run or we'll miss the bus."

"Goodbye, Mrs. Jones," we chorused.

"It has been a pleasure to meet you, madam." Mr. Schmidt gave Mrs. Jones his most charming, knee-buckling smile and held out his hand for Mrs. Jones to shake. She simpered girlishly.

"The pleasure is mine, Mr. Smith." She put her hand in his and smiled up at him. "Do I detect an accent?"

"Indeed you do, Mrs. Jones. How clever of you. Yes, I am from Switzerland but my parents were from England. Three years ago, I came to your wonderful country to teach. I have always considered it my real home because of my parentage. And the people—just like you—are so friendly and welcoming."

Mr. Schmidt kept hold of Mrs. Jones' hand. His voice was soft and warm and he continued to gaze into her eyes. What I would have given to be in Mrs. Jones' place!

"But now, alas, we must go. Can't miss the bus, can we? I do hope to see you again soon." He freed his hand, bowed his head slightly, and smiled as we made our departure.

I glanced at Esther, who looked like she might explode with laughter. When we were a safe distance from Mrs. Jones, we collapsed into giggles.

"Oh, Henry," Esther chortled, wiping a tear from her eye, "you were magnificent. I could never imagine anyone flirting so deliberately with Mrs. Jones. She's old enough to be your grandmother."

"I? Flirt?" Mr. Schmidt said, his voice innocent but his eyes twinkling. "I would never flirt. I don't know the meaning of the word."

Esther turned her attention to Quigs. "I wonder what relation you actually are. I suppose nephew will do, although Fred doesn't have any brothers or sisters. You must be a second cousin, or something. Well, it doesn't make any difference. You're obviously a Quigley, and you're here to stay."

"Yes," said Quigley, "I'm here to stay. If you'll have me."

He looked past Esther to Mr. Schmidt, Marina, and me and winked broadly. My heart sank. Quigs certainly had his feet under the table and he had no intention of removing them. How on earth were we going to get him to come back to the twenty-first century?

)))

We went into shop after shop, buying socks and underclothes in one and blouses, skirts, shirts and shorts in another; a suit for Mr. Schmidt; knitting wool for a new sweater for Joseph; a hat for Esther—the list went on and on. Esther was a most efficient shopper, alternating between steely determination and coy flirtatiousness, whatever she thought would get the best possible price out of each shopkeeper. Our expedition over, Mr. Schmidt carried Joseph to the bus stop on his shoulders to stop him from whining.

"Now, Henry, if you and the girls and Joseph can drop this little lot off at home, Quigs and I'll stay on the bus until we get to Penge to get something for tea. I should really have gone there earlier. I hope there's something left at the butchers'. Quigs, later on, would you mind going to the caretaker's at the school and asking Herbert Martin to come and get a rabbit this evening? Then I can have a nice dinner waiting for you when you come home from school tomorrow."

We piled onto the crowded bus. I squashed in beside an old man who smelled disagreeably of a mixture of tobacco, beer, and cabbage. He belched loudly and gave me a wink and a toothless leer. Mr. Schmidt, standing beside me, froze the man with a cold glare and put a protective hand on my shoulder. The old man mumbled an apology and gazed fixedly out of the window.

Despite the nasty old man, I was quite sorry to reach our bus stop. I had drifted off into a reverie about Mr. Schmidt being my knight in shining armor, protecting me from all sorts of nasty old men, when Esther gave me a poke from behind. "Go on, dreamer, this is your stop. Off you go!"

I jumped up, blushing. Still flustered, I leaped off the bus and bumped straight into a tall, thin boy about my age.

"Sorry!" I gasped, staring into two icy, pale-blue eyes. I had only ever seen eyes of that color and intensity on one other person.

"Mr. Martin?"

"Well, most people call me Bert, but you can call me Mr. Martin if you like." He grinned, looking over my shoulder. "In fact, you can call me anything at all, as long as you introduce me to your friend."

My face burning, I grabbed Marina's arm and dragged her forward.

"Hello! I'm Marina Curtis. Nice to meet you. We're staying with Mrs. Quigley for a while, because we were bombed out. You're the school caretaker's son, I believe?"

I escaped and caught up with Mr. Schmidt, who walked on ahead, once again carrying Joseph on his shoulders.

"Henry!" I puffed. "Did you see that boy's eyes? Have you ever seen another pair of eyes like that?"

Mr. Schmidt smiled down at me. "Well, I must confess I didn't notice his eyes. But then, I'm not an adolescent girl and I didn't nearly knock him down."

"No, listen. Don't you remember Mr. Martin's eyes? How they were that pale, creepy, cold blue color? Well, that Bert Martin has those same eyes. Sir, it has to be Mr. Martin. He must be the key to getting us home."

"Good afternoon, Mrs. Jones!" Mr. Schmidt called out to our nosy neighbor who just happened to be shaking her duster out of the upstairs window as we passed.

"Good afternoon, Mr. Smith," she cooed back. "You seem to have bought half of Beckenham."

He laughed obligingly, and then whispered, "Say good afternoon, Sophie. Remember your manners."

"Good afternoon, Mrs. Jones," I repeated obediently. Then softly, impatiently, "Come on, sir. We have to figure out a plan."

We waved dutifully to Mrs. Jones, and Mr. Schmidt gave his courtly little bow. Joseph, hanging on to Mr. Schmidt's hair, shrieked with laughter. Mrs. Jones practically swooned as she closed the window.

Mr. Schmidt turned and smiled as Marina and Bert caught up to us. "Ah, Marina! How slowly you have walked. Perhaps you could introduce me to your friend."

"Sir, this is Bert Martin. His dad is the caretaker at the school. Bert, this is Mr. Smith."

Mr. Schmidt was about to shake Bert's hand when the air-raid siren gave its warning wail. Joseph let out a howl of his own.

"Well, Bert, would you care to share our shelter with us?" Mr. Schmidt asked.

"Great!" he agreed, grinning at Marina.

"What about Esther and Quigs?" I tugged at Mr. Schmidt's arm urgently.

"Ah, don't worry about them," Bert replied. "Lots of places to shelter on the High Street. You don't think the shop owners want all their customers blown to smithereens, do you? Bad for business."

We ducked into the shelter as the first line of planes went overhead. "Maybe they'll give us a miss and go on to the city center this time," Bert said hopefully.

"There are people up there too," I protested.

"Yeah, sorry. Marina told me that your parents had—been killed." Bert looked uncomfortable, his icy eyes clouding over.

Joseph gave great, gulping sobs, demanding his mother. I trudged up and down the shelter with him on my hip, stepping over everyone's feet.

"So, Bert. Why aren't you in school today? It is only two o'clock. Are you unwell?" Trust Mr. Schmidt to take attendance before he'd even started at the school.

"Dunno. Didn't want to go. French. Hate it."

"Oh, dear. That is a shame. Because starting tomorrow, I will be your French teacher, and I will expect you to be in school. All lessons are necessary if you wish to get a good job in the future."

A giggle rose in my throat at the thought of Mr. Schmidt telling old Mr. Martin to behave.

Mr. Schmidt continued, "Or don't you care about the future?"

The cacophony of the aircraft overhead and Joseph's bawling nearly drowned out Mr. Schmidt's question. In a sudden lull in the din, Bert lifted his head, looked Mr. Schmidt straight in the eye, and said: "You should leave the future alone. It will come by itself. Just leave the future alone."

You could have heard a pin drop.

Marina's green eyes met mine. We both looked at Mr. Schmidt.

"Why do you say that, Bert? Why don't you care about the future?"

"What's to care about in the past or in the future? The past is dead. Leave it alone. The future will come by itself, with no interference from us." He almost spat the words out. "So leave it alone."

He opened the shelter door.

"Bert!" Marina shouted, holding out her hand. "Don't go out there. You could get killed!"

From the distance came the dull explosion of bombs.

Bert looked at us one by one, his eyes calm. "No. No, I won't. You know that."

He softly shut the door behind him.

"Sir, he knows, doesn't he? He knows who we are and where we're from." Marina's voice shook.

Mr. Schmidt shrugged. "Who knows? Maybe he knows and maybe he doesn't. Twelve-year-old boys are odd, to say the least. He might have said that we know he won't die merely to be dramatic. And he did sympathize with you about the death of your parents. Would he have said that if he'd known we were from the future? So, we have to assume he doesn't know. He has the same attitude to the future as our Mr. Martin had to the past, that's for sure, and Sophie was quite right about his eyes. Well done, Sophie."

Blushing, I looked up from the Snakes and Ladders game I was trying to interest Joseph in, and smiled. "It would be pretty hard to miss them, sir." I rolled a six and moved my piece up a ladder.

"Here, give me a counter; I'll play, too. Marina?" She nodded. "But we have to figure out how he can help us get back to the twenty-first century, *if* he can." He slid down a snake. "Ah! Back to the beginning." He tapped the dice thoughtfully on the board. "Back to the beginning," he repeated, slowly. "That is what we must do. Go back to the beginning. I think we'll have to recreate what brought us here in the first place."

"My turn!" Joseph shouted, holding out his pudgy hand for the dice. "Eleventy-seven!" he announced triumphantly.

I helped him move his counter four places, and slid him up a ladder.

"Well, that should be easy enough, Henry," Marina commented, cleaning her glasses on her skirt. "We just have to go down the air-raid shelter and come up again. Presto change-o! Back to normal."

"Hmmm, will it be so easy?" Mr. Schmidt wondered, moving two places. "Can it really be so very easy?"

)))

"Marina got a new boyfriend today," I said wickedly, winking at Esther behind Marina's back. "That caretaker's son. Bert Martin."

Esther waved a small parcel wrapped in waxy, brown paper in the air. "A special day all round, then! I actually got some chops. How's that for a stroke of luck? The last ones in the shop. Blimey, I didn't half have to bill and coo at the butcher to get them." She pulled a face at the memory. "So, Bert's taken with Marina, is he?"

"Boys always like Marina," I said. "They always have, and always will."

Esther laughed. "So much for boys not making passes at girls who wear glasses. He's quite a nice boy, though. Helpful. Though, I don't know, there's something a bit . . . not odd, exactly . . . different about him. Maybe it's those eyes."

"Do his parents have those bright blue eyes, too?" Marina asked casually, keeping her eyes on the peas she was shelling.

"No, strangely. They both have brown eyes. He must be a throwback or something."

"He just left the shelter in the middle of the raid. I suppose he was bored with us," Marina said.

"Well, that's Bert for you. His parents have given up trying to get him to stay in the air-raid shelter. I think he figures if a bomb doesn't have his name written on it, he won't get hit. Let's hope he doesn't find out otherwise. Here, are you finished with those peas? Good girl. Quigs, go and give the empty pods to the rabbits, please. Marina, when you saw Bert, did you ask him to do a rabbit for us?"

"No, sorry; I completely forgot. Do you want me to go over and ask him? If Quigs comes, then I can introduce him. That way, he'll know someone at school tomorrow."

"Marina, you don't actually like him, do you?" I whispered, as Esther vanished into the pantry.

"Of course I like him; he's all right."

"I mean *like* him, like him. Mr. Martin. He's seventy-five, at least."

"Well, if it comes to that, so am I. And so are you. And I don't even want to think how old Mr. Schmidt is."

She had a point. Not a very nice point to think about, but a point, nonetheless.

"Anyway, it's not like I'm going to marry him or anything. Good grief, I'm only eleven—no wait, I'd be twelve. I was born on September second, so I guess I'm twelve now. Huh! Fancy that."

"What are you two whispering about?" Esther smiled as she came out of the pantry. "Young Master Martin, no doubt. Oh yes, I remember being your age. Whispers and giggles." She gazed wistfully out the window, her hand on her tummy. "Giggle while you can."

A single aircraft flew over the house. "Blimey, that's a bit low," shouted Quigs, charging outside. "Look! It's coming round again. It's a Spitfire!"

We ran out, staring up at the sky. The small plane came around again and did a barrel roll as it skimmed the chimneys.

"Fred!" Esther screamed, jumping up and down, waving. She picked up Joseph and held him in her arms, pointing up at the sky. "Joseph! That's your Daddy! Look, here he comes again."

Once more, the plane buzzed the rooftops. After climbing steeply, it rolled twice, and flew off towards the southeast.

"Fred, oh Fred." Tears streamed down Esther's cheeks. Joseph tried to wipe them away with his hands.

"Don't cry, Mummy. Don't cry."

"Come, children." Mr. Schmidt ushered us into the house. "Leave them be."

We stood at the window and watched Esther and Joseph stare into the distance.

"That's it," Quigs said fiercely. "That's it. I'm going to find Fred and bring him back."

"You can't!" Mr. Schmidt, Marina, and I said as one.

"Oh, can't I? Just watch me. I'm going to bring Fred home if it's the last thing I do."

CHAPTER 5

》》》 Tuesday, September 17, 1940

Warmly snuggled underneath the blankets, I dreamed of a time when I could sleep the whole night through without having to take a stroll to a giant tin can at the back of the garden. The alarm clock jangled in my right ear. I swiped my hand in that general direction and knocked the clock off the nightstand to the floor, where its clamor continued.

Grumbling under my breath, I tumbled out of bed, turned off the alarm, and whacked Marina with my pillow.

"Don't tell me it's morning already. Or is it another stupid raid? Are there going to be raids every single night?"

"Henry told me last night that London was bombed every night for something like fifty-seven nights, right up to December, I think. So I suppose we'd better get used to it. Maybe we should start off in the shelter, and not bother going in and out. Or out and in. Whichever."

I opened the curtains. Rain. Torrents of it. Wonderful. I was going to start school looking like a drowned rat.

I tied the belt of my robe—well, Esther's old robe—around my waist and headed downstairs. Quigs came out of his room as I passed his door.

"Has anyone ever told you that you're truly beautiful first thing in the morning, Sophie?"

"Well, at least I know I'll improve when I've combed my hair and washed my face, which is more than I can say for you, Quigley. And don't insult a girl when you're standing in front of her at the top of a long flight of stairs, and she has her hand on your back, ready to push."

He rattled down the stairs with me in hot pursuit.

"Morning!" Esther turned around from making toast. "Only toast today, I'm afraid. No milk for cereal; the milkman didn't come. Henry's gone already, said he wanted to prepare his lessons. He left some money for your school meals on the table."

"Will you be okay by yourself today?" Quigs asked, stuffing toast into his face. "What if there's another raid?"

"Quigs, sweetie, you're lovely to worry about me, but remember, until day before yesterday, Joseph and I had been here by ourselves since the beginning of the war. More or less, anyway. I'll think we'll manage." Esther ruffled Quigs' hair as she walked by. "Oooh! When did you last wash your hair, young man? It's disgusting!" She laughed and wiped her hand on her apron.

"Dunno. Last Wednesday, I think."

"Come here. I am not having people say my nephew is a ragamuffin." She grabbed Quigs firmly by the ear, and shoved his head under the kitchen tap. Marina walked in to the sound of Quigs howling as Esther soaped his hair, rinsed it, and rubbed it dry with a towel.

"There! That's better! Didn't take long, did it?"

"Blimey, do I have any hair left or did you rub it all off?" He gingerly felt the top of his head.

Esther grinned and hugged him. My jaw dropped when he kissed her on the cheek and hugged her back. "That'll teach you to take care of your own personal hygiene, Master Quigley," she said. "Soap might be in short supply, but it isn't nonexistent. Well, not yet anyway. You could have lubricated Fred's Spitfire with the grease on your head. You all had better get a move on. You can't be late on your first day. I can get Joseph up and come with you, if you like."

"No, we'll be fine," Marina assured her. "We're looking forward to it, aren't we, Sophie?"

I mumbled a noncommittal reply and fiddled with my toast. Marina might be looking forward to going to school, but I was terrified. What if the curriculum was so different that I didn't know anything? Well, geography would certainly be different. I was sure all the countries in Africa had been renamed since the war. But considering I didn't know their names in my own time, this might be a blessing in disguise. And what if nobody liked me? I always worried about that. It was fine for Marina; she was always popular. But I tended to fade into the background, and now I'd have to meet a whole new bunch of people, some of whom could possibly be the grandmas of the people I should be going to school with. And what if, most horribly of all, I let it slip that I belonged in a different time?

"Are you eating that toast or sculpting it?" Esther asked.

"Sorry." I jammed the toast into my mouth and took my plate to the sink.

"Leave the plates. But get a move on, girl." Her voice wasn't unkind, and her eyes were sympathetic. I think she understood how I felt, if not why. I gave her a hug.

"Oh, Esther, what would we have done without you?"

I turned and ran up the stairs.

〉〉〉

Heads down against the thin drizzle, we joined a long crocodile of girls making their way towards the school. "And didn't he look a sight for sore eyes going to school?" Marina still giggled about Quigs' experience in the kitchen "Those shorts! And that raincoat! And the cap!" She let out another ear-piercing shriek of laughter.

"Hello, there! What's the joke? I need a good laugh. Didn't get my essay done, so good humor will be in short supply for me at school." A plump, jolly girl with mousy hair and freckles joined us. "Don't think we've met. My name is Pru. How do you do?"

I left the introductions to Marina and did my mental disappearing act. I was reflecting on how handy it was to be able to sort of fold myself up inside, when Pru put her arm across my shoulders and gave me a firm squeeze.

"Hard luck, old thing. Simply beastly about your parents and your home and everything. Ghastly war. Here we are! Come on! I'll show you to the office and introduce you to Miss Stanley. Not a bad old bean as headmistresses go. Mind you, she's got a voice that can shatter glass at fifty paces, so if she gives you a tongue-lashing the entire school knows about it. No, strike that, the entire communities of Penge, Beckenham and Sydenham know. Don't know why they don't pop her on top of the police station and use her as an air-raid siren."

I relaxed and laughed despite myself. Pru pushed open the heavy doors and marched us into the office. "Hello, Mrs. Johnson," she greeted a frail-looking woman banging away on a huge, black typewriter. "Got a couple of new victims—oops, pupils—to see Miss Stanley. Is she in?"

Mrs. Johnson looked up and gave a friendly smile. "Good morning, girls. I see you've met our Prudence. Never mind. Not all the girls are like her."

"No, some are even worse," said Pru, laughing. "Oops, snap to attention, ladies. Here comes Miss Stanley."

My heart dropped. Miss Stanley appeared to be a carbon copy of Miss Pratt—tall, thin, and elegant. Was there a factory where they turned out these women? I imagined them coming off the assembly line like biscuits.

"Are you deaf, girl? I said good morning."

My face burned. "Sorry, Miss Stanley. I—I was thinking about—about the last time I went to school—" I stumbled over the words, trying to think of a reasonable excuse; I couldn't very well tell her the picture in my mind.

Marina came to my rescue. "The last time we went to school, we had parents to go home to at the end of the day. Mrs. Quigley is very kind, but she's not our mother." Behind her glasses, she balanced tears on the ends of her eyelashes, a trick she had learned long ago would melt a heart of stone. I could see Miss Stanley's heart dissolving before my very eyes.

Miss Stanley smiled gently and patted our shoulders. "I'm so sorry about your loss and I'm sure everyone here will be kind and supportive. I've put you two in the same class; I thought you might appreciate knowing someone. It's never easy on one's first day of school, even more so under these circumstances. Prudence is a prefect, so she can show you the way, and will look after you for the first few days. She's three years ahead of you—in the Fourth Form—and so is quite sensible. Aren't you, Prudence?" She looked at Pru sternly over the tops of her glasses. "I suppose your records were lost in the bombing, so we'll have to start from scratch. Therefore, whatever you were like in your old school, this is a completely new beginning for you. You're dismissed." She looked pointedly at me. I think she had gathered that Marina simply oozed brains, and had probably marked me down as being mentally deficient. Still, that was okay; I didn't have to live up to any expectations, and if I didn't prove to be a complete idiot, everyone—including myself—would be pleasantly surprised.

> > >

Actually, the morning wasn't as bad as I thought it was going to be. Assembly was not much different from what I was used to. Mrs. Johnson took a break from banging out letters on her typewriter and banged out "God Save the King" and a hymn about Those in Peril on the Sea on an ancient piano instead. Miss Stanley had made Marina and me stand up to officially welcome us to the school. Marina had sailed through it, of course, but I'd wished the ground would swallow me. I didn't like telling people my parents were dead; it made me feel creepy. After Assembly came history and English, which had always been my two favorite subjects, because they allowed my imagination to run riot. At least I hadn't disgraced myself academically, for which I was truly grateful.

Nevertheless, I was glad when lunchtime rolled around. Pru found us in the classroom. "You can sit at my table," she invited. "I've got two empty spots because the Watson sisters moved down to Cornwall over the holiday."

We filed into the dining hall and stood behind our chairs. Miss Stanley and the teachers sat at a long table at the front of the hall. Miss Stanley stood and intoned, "For what we are about to receive, may the Lord make us truly thankful. Amen." I looked down at the bowls of congealing gray stew, lumpy gray potatoes and dried gray peas placed in the middle of the table. I thought we needed the Lord's intervention, because under no other circumstances could anyone be grateful for this.

"Did we honestly complain about the food at our school last week?" Marina murmured. "And does this come out of our rations? Because if it does, I want a refund."

"Close your eyes. Chew. Swallow. Sit back and think of England," I suggested. I was quite good at that, having had a lot of practice. I'd never been sure why Dad had left Mum and married Sylvia, but it certainly hadn't been for Sylvia's cooking, though even her food looked better than this.

"Come on, girls!" Pru encouraged us. "Take the gravy—with the emphasis on grave—rather than the meat. Shove it on your spuds and mush it up. And remember, we have lumpy gray rice pudding to look forward to."

The cook, a sour-looking woman who carried a large ladle as though it was a weapon, plodded around the dining hall. She chided girls here and there for playing with their food. "Be grateful for what you have. Don't you know there's a war on?"

This fact—of which we were only too aware—was suddenly emphasized by the sound of the air-raid siren. "Saved by the bell," Marina whispered. "Thank you, Mr. Hitler, wherever you may be."

"What was that you said?" The cook's voice hissed in my ear. "Did you say 'Thank you, Mr. Hitler'?"

I tried to stammer a reply, but nothing came out.

"I'm so sorry, Cook," Marina smiled apologetically at the angry woman. "It wasn't Sophie; it was me. I think you may have misunderstood my meaning. I was trying to be sarcastic, but obviously, it didn't come out that way. I mean, of all the times to have an air raid—right in the middle of our lovely meal!"

The cook looked at her doubtfully. I could tell she wanted to believe this pretty girl with the big green eyes, but she was loathe to back down.

She snorted. "Right then. Better get down to the shelter. Your food will still be here when you get out." She stomped off.

"Come along, girls! Smartly!" Miss Stanley came up behind us. "Now then, were you upsetting Cook?"

"Oh, I do hope not, Miss Stanley," Marina replied virtuously. "I was so enjoying my stew."

Miss Stanley stared at her. "Just how bad was the food at your old school, if you were enjoying that?" She walked off, smiling. Funny how teachers surprise you sometimes.

A tall, thin girl with straggly hair pinched Marina hard as we entered the shelter. Under her breath, she said: "You may have fooled Cook and Miss Stanley, but I heard you. You definitely said 'Thank you, Mr. Hitler.' And it wasn't said sarcastically; not at all. I've heard the Germans use nuns as spies, so why not schoolgirls? Who on earth would suspect you two? Well, I've got your number, make no mistake about it. I'll be watching you."

Pru called us from across the room. "Come on, girls! I've saved you some seats. We can have a nice little chat while old Jerry does his worst up there."

The straggly-haired girl's eyes bored into my back as we hurried over. Had Marina's remark put all of us—not only Marina, Quigs, Mr. Schmidt and me, but also Esther and Joseph—in danger? Would we be arrested as spies? And would Esther be arrested for harboring us? And if so, what would happen to Joseph?

Marina squeezed my hand. "Don't worry. We'll be all right."

But Marina sounded as worried as I felt. What on earth would happen now?

)))

True to her word, Esther had cooked the rabbit. Although I wanted to heave at the thought of eating a rabbit, I had to admit it smelled delicious.

"Don't get used to having meals like this," Esther said as she passed the plates. "This is only because it's a special occasion. I expect the school meals will keep you going, with only a light tea when you get back."

I couldn't tell her how awful the food was at school, so I smiled and said, "Oh yes, I'm sure they will. They give us so much."

Quigs nodded in agreement. "The food at my school is super! Much better than it used to be when I was there before."

I caught my breath. Esther looked puzzled.

"I mean, better than it was in my old school. In the East End. Pass the peas, please."

"So how did the children treat you, Henry? Did they like their new teacher?" Esther asked, as she passed Quigs the peas.

"Well, except for one little hiccup," he replied, helping himself to potatoes. "But it was nothing, really."

"Was not!" Quigs answered vehemently. "You were brilliant. Out in the playground, some of the boys called Henry a Nazi because of his accent. So he told them he was Swiss, and they called him a liar. They said he was a Nazi spy, and that they would be watching him."

I felt the blood drain from my face.

Quigs continued, "So, then—may I have some gravy, please?—one of the other teachers comes up, and asks what's going on, and Henry wouldn't tell him, so I told him. Then, the other teacher said Henry had to cane the boys for rudeness. So Henry says, 'If I were to beat them with a cane, sir, then I would be no better than the Nazi they think I am. They have the right to their opinion and the right to express it.'" Quigs even did Mr. Schmidt's accent perfectly. "And Henry said that he knew he wasn't a Nazi, and they would have to accept what he said was true until they proved it to themselves. And some of the boys who were standing and listening, even applauded him. This is great, Esther! I never knew rabbits tasted so good."

Marina and I exchanged glances across the table. So, people were watching us everywhere. The neighbors' curtains twitched wildly every time we walked down the street, the straggly-haired girl had her eye on us, and now Mr. Schmidt's pupils were suspicious of him. I was sure the axe would fall eventually—but when?

CHAPTER 6

))) Wednesday, September 18, 1940

Mr. Schmidt, Marina, Quigs, and I stood on the back doorstep and watched Lewisham and Deptford burn in the distance. While Esther readied Joseph for bed, I'd taken the opportunity to tell Mr. Schmidt and Quigs about the straggly-haired girl, making a mental note to find out her name.

Mr. Schmidt sighed heavily. *"Ja,* it would certainly appear we have to devise a method to get back sooner rather than later. It would only take one investigation into our background, or rather our lack of background, to convince everyone I really am a Nazi and have somehow inveigled you into my evil plan. And Quigs, don't start on your 'I want to stay here' speech. I know you do, and I do understand the reasons why. But we cannot stay a minute longer than is absolutely necessary. And yes, you do have to come back with us. It would be most difficult to explain to your parents how I managed to lose you without having left the school grounds."

"You can say I ran away or was kidnapped or something. I don't really care what story you tell."

"Don't be ridiculous. Despite what you think, your parents must love you. No, we will make arrangements to go back—tomorrow night. You must do as I say, and follow my lead."

"But what about Esther?" I whispered. "Aren't we even going to leave her a note?"

"And say what? 'Oh, sorry, had to go back to the twenty-first century'?" Mr. Schmidt's harsh tone surprised me. He sighed and continued more softly. "But, no, you are right. We can't merely disappear. I shall leave her a note with the money I have and say you had missed the East End and wanted to live with relatives there. I'll leave it in your room, girls, so she will not find it too quickly."

"I'm not going," Quigs muttered. "You can't make me." He looked up, and in the dull glow from the moon, I could see tears in his eyes and a look of anguish on his face.

Mr. Schmidt put his arm around Quigs' shoulders. "Quigs, sometimes we have to do things that are very, very hard for us. Things that we do not want to do. Things that make us feel our heart will break. But we do them because it is right to do them. And going back to our own time is the right thing for us to do."

For a fraction of a second, Quigs turned his head and rested his face against Mr. Schmidt's jacket. Then he pulled away and marched into the house.

"Come, girls," Mr. Schmidt said in the same heavy tone. "You must try to get some sleep. Rest up for your last day in 1940."

)))

"Hello, girls!" Pru's cheerful voice rang out. "Whew! I'm all out of breath trying to catch up with you. You do walk fast. Can't believe you're in such a rush to get to school. Did you get much sleep last night?"

"Not too bad," Marina replied. "We went to bed quite early, so we got quite a lot of rest before the raid. Stood outside and watched the fires afterwards."

Pru nodded. "My aunt got bombed last night. Well, two doors down from her took the hit, but her windows got blown out. Let's hope there's never a glass shortage. Oh, what does Gert want?"

The straggly-haired girl was walking straight toward us, her lips sewn into a thin line and her eyebrows knitted into a scowl.

Pru called out, "Gert, careful, your face will freeze that way. Why on earth are you glowering like that?"

"Those two girls you're with," Gert replied. "Those two. German sympathizers. I'd stay clear of them if I was you, or it'll probably be your house bombed next."

Pru laughed. "What a load of rubbish, Gert! German sympathizers, indeed. They were bombed out by the Jerries, you know that."

"Do I?" Gert replied darkly. "I don't know that, and neither do you. No one does. You only take their word for it. You trust everyone; all in it together. Smile nicely and be good neighbors. Well, Hitler's not a good neighbour and neither are these two. Remember, careless talk costs lives."

She stalked off, her hair hanging like rats' tails around her face.

"I don't know what gets into that girl, I really don't," Pru declared. "She's been weird ever since she was five. Don't look so upset. No one would ever believe a word she says."

I shivered as a cold gust of wind whipped down the street, swirling leaves around my ankles. A solitary plane buzzed overhead—a German plane.

Gert turned around. "Your friends have come to say hello!" she shouted back at us. "Aren't you going to give them a wave?"

The plane banked and flew east.

"Ah, shame, they're going home without you," said the taunting voice.

Marina laid a warning hand on my arm as I bent to pick up a horse chestnut to throw at Gert. "Don't lower yourself to her level," she whispered. "Just ignore her. She'll go away."

I took a deep breath and swallowed. Well, someone would be going away, I thought, and hopefully it would be Marina and me. Tonight.

)))

The day dragged interminably, with the first air-raid siren not sounding until after lunch.

I had mixed feelings about the raid. It had rescued me from domestic science, in which the rest of the class was knitting socks for soldiers. My grandmother had tried to teach me to knit once, but with a singular lack of success. My fingers simply couldn't get the rhythm of in, round, through, out. Mrs. Thorpe, the teacher, had stared at me in amazement when I'd confessed that at the ripe old age of eleven-and-three-quarters I still couldn't do so much as cast on. She set me the humiliating task of unraveling old school sweaters to reuse the wool.

On the other hand, I knew Marina and I would be treated to Gert's evil eye in the air-raid shelter. We tried to stay as far away from her as possible and sat close to Miss Stanley. Even Gert wouldn't dare to hurl accusations at us in front of Miss Stanley—well, I hoped not, anyway.

The raid was mercifully short, but long enough to allow the knitting class to end. The rest of the day passed in even more of a blur than is usual for me. All I could think about was how in a few hours time I might be in my proper place and my proper time.

》 》 》

"Exactly why are we doing this homework, Marina?" I asked, as we sat at the kitchen table with our books in front of us. "We're going home tonight."

"You know that for sure, do you?" she said, dipping her pen in the inkpot. "What if it doesn't work? Actually, when you think about it, why should it work?"

"Well, because . . . because . . . Mr. Schmidt said it would." I sighed as I made a huge blot the shape of Great Britain on my mathematics book.

Marina drew a neat line under her math homework. "He hopes it will. And so do I. But we have to be realistic."

Quigs burst into the kitchen carrying Joseph piggyback. "Realistic about what?" he puffed, galloping around the kitchen.

"Getting back, of course."

"Faster, horsey, faster!" Joseph commanded.

Quigs neighed loudly, and pawed at the air with his hands.

"Nope. Won't work. Not going back. Hey, kid, are you trying to strangle your horsey?" With a whinny from Quigs and a "Giddy-up!" from Joseph, the pair charged into the garden.

"Have you ever seen Quigs so happy?" I asked.

Marina sucked thoughtfully on her pen. "No, no. I haven't. It's a shame. He's finally found happiness, and it's going to be over before it's begun."

Esther stuck her head through the door. "Is it all right if I start making the tea? Got some sort of, nearly, pretend sausages today. Not sure what's in them, which is probably for the best. Sawdust if we're lucky!" I tried to concentrate on her pleasant chatter. I hoped she wouldn't be too sad to find we had disappeared. She'd done so much for us, and we intended to repay her kindness by leaving without even saying goodbye. "Are you crying again, Sophie girl? The sausages won't be that bad! Come on, give me a hug."

I jumped up and hugged her hard. Marina came over and wrapped her arms around both of us.

Quigs and Joseph cantered back into the kitchen.

"Group hug!" Quigs shouted, and with Joseph still on his back, joined the huddle.

Mr. Schmidt walked in, laughing.

"What is going on here? Are you trying to suffocate poor Esther?"

"No, only trying to stop her from cooking sawdust sausages," I replied, freeing myself.

"Hmmm, sounds appetizing. Now, give Esther a hand with the tea, and make sure your homework is completed."

I met his eyes, which seemed tinged with sadness. How odd; I thought he couldn't wait to go home again.

〉〉〉

The sound of a lullaby drifted down the stairs as Esther settled Joseph into bed. I dried the last plate and placed it in the cupboard.

Mr. Schmidt sighed. "Right, children, this is it. I have left a note on the mantel in the girls' bedroom for Esther, thanking her for all she has done. We had better leave while she is upstairs. And Quigs, wipe that mutinous look off your face. Deep inside, you know this is the right thing to do. We will always have memories of our short time here. So, come on."

We crept quietly out of the house, making sure to shut the door very gently. I heard a telltale sniff from Quigs.

"Getting a cold," he mumbled.

Mr. Schmidt knocked on the door of the caretaker's quarters at the school. I looked around the grounds. This was the first time I had returned to the school since Sunday. It was strange—everything was obviously newer than it was in the twenty-first century, but appeared older, drabber. No bright murals were painted on the high brick wall down by the nursery-school building. Actually, the nursery-school building wasn't even there. The tall ginkgo tree, whose bright yellow leaves the girls made into little posies in the autumn, was a frail sapling. And instead of the Eurostar train to Paris humming by, a steam train puffed its way over the bridge.

The flat door opened. Herbert Martin stood in the doorway, a guarded look in his frosty eyes.

Mr. Schmidt cleared his throat. "Ah, good evening, Bert. I was wondering if you could give us a hand. On Sunday, Marina dropped her bracelet in the air-raid shelter. It was the only remembrance she had of her mother, and she is heartbroken."

Bert's eyes drifted over to Marina, who turned pink.

"Would you be so kind as to come with us to the shelter and help us look for it? I know Marina would be most grateful."

Marina fluttered her green eyes at Bert.

Bert picked up a large torch from the shelf beside the door. "Won't work, you know."

Mr. Schmidt inhaled sharply. "What won't work?'

"Finding the bracelet, of course. Blimey, someone's stolen it by now, I should think."

"It might have fallen in a corner, beside the wall," Marina suggested. "Maybe no one saw it."

Bert shrugged. "Dunno. But I say it won't work."

Mr. Schmidt walked behind the group, his hand firmly on Quigs' shoulder. A shiver ran down my spine as we reached the shelter. "Goodbye, 1940," I murmured, taking a last look around before following Bert down the stairs into the darkness.

Mr. Schmidt shut the shelter door behind us.

"No need for that," said Bert. "There's not a raid on and it's daylight." He turned on the electric lights and flipped off the torch. "Right, Marina, where do you think you dropped it?"

Before Marina had a chance to reply, the lights flickered and died, leaving us in the same pitch black we'd been in when this whole time-portal thing started. This must be it. We were heading back to our own time. But how long would we have to stay here in the dark?

I couldn't stand the suspense. I ran up the stairs, flung open the door, and peered back down into the shelter. Marina, Quigs, and Mr. Schmidt stood in the faint glow of light from the doorway—but where was Bert Martin?

Bert had gone. Vanished. Disappeared.

"Bert?" I quavered. "Mr. Martin?"

I crept slowly down the stairs again.

"I told you that you didn't have to call me Mr. Martin," Bert teased, as he reappeared from behind the stairs.

I gasped. "Where . . . where were you? I—I thought—"

Did I imagine the faintly sympathetic light in his eyes? "You thought, did you?" he mocked. "It isn't good to think. I was only fixing the fuse. Has a nasty habit of blowing. There!"

The lights snapped back on.

The sound of bombers filled the air.

It hadn't worked. We were still trapped in 1940.

"So, do you want to look for the bracelet?"

"No," Marina replied, dully. "No, you were right. It didn't work. Come on, let's go."

Outside, Quigs raced down the path, arms out like an airplane, roaring and ratatatat-ing.

"How much do you know, Bert Martin?" Mr. Schmidt asked quietly.

"Me? Know? What do you mean?" His blue eyes glistened like icicles. "All I know is, it doesn't pay to think, and it doesn't pay to mess around with things you don't understand." He paused. "Like those French verbs you gave us, sir. I simply don't understand them." His eyes were serene, and his mouth, slightly mocking.

"Well, come over to the house, then. I'll be glad to explain them to you." Mr. Schmidt turned and walked away with Marina and me. As we walked on, Bert Martin's piercing gaze burned holes in my back.

"So, we're trapped here, sir." Marina sounded like she might cry. "We're never going home again, are we?"

Mr. Schmidt didn't reply. He laid his arms across our shoulders and sighed deeply. We walked back home to the only home we might ever know, to Esther's house.

CHAPTER 7

))) Thursday, September 19, 1940

"It's good we did our homework," Marina said, as we walked to school the next morning. "I don't think the teachers would accept 'I thought I was going to do a little time-travel' as a reasonable excuse."

"I really, really thought it would work. Quigs is happy, though. And at least we got back before Esther discovered the note. Oh, Marina, do you think we'll ever get back home?"

"I don't know. Back in our time, they must be tearing that shelter apart looking for us or for clues. Probably digging up the floor." Marina stopped dead and grabbed my arm. "Soph, do you think that's what the problem is? We can't get back because the police have damaged the shelter too much? In that case, we'll never get back."

We stared at each other in horror.

Pru ran up behind us. "Hello, chums! I've been calling you for ages, but you were deep in conversation. Blimey, what on earth is wrong with you two? You look like you've lost a pound and found a sixpence."

"I—um—just remembered some homework I forgot to do," I stammered.

"Well, if we get a move on, you can do it before school starts. I'll give you a hand. Well, so long as it isn't math. Not my best subject. Not even First Form math. Oh, no, there's Gert. I hope she's not going to start that stupid German sympathizer bit again. It's getting a bit tedious. If she carries on, I'll tell Miss Stanley. Blimey, that plane's a bit low!"

We gasped as a small German plane swooped over the houses and flew straight down the street towards us. "Hit the ground!" Pru shouted, as the staccato rattle of machine-gun fire hammered out. "Sophie, get down!"

Around me, girls dove under bushes and behind walls, but I couldn't move. I stood transfixed by the giant nightmarish daisy of the plane's bright yellow nosecone and whirling propeller. I vaguely heard Marina scream my name, but I stayed rooted to the spot. The street pirouetted madly around me.

"Sophie!" Marina shrieked desperately.

The plane crawled through the sky toward me. Gunfire clattered all around. Something like a ten-ton truck struck me from behind. A burning, searing pain blazed through me. The world went black.

》 》 》

"Help me take that coat off her. Here, give me your tie. No, I can't use mine; can't you see I've got both hands full trying to stop the bleeding? Selfish little horror. Oh, not you, Soph!" Pru said, as my eyes flickered open. "That toad, Gert. Standing over you like the flipping Angel of Death. What on earth were you thinking, providing target practice like that? You would have looked like a tea strainer by now if Marina hadn't tackled you from behind. Here, Marina, fasten your tie tightly around her arm, right above the bleeding. That's good. Anyone have a ruler? Come on, you lazy lot, someone must have one. Thanks."

I flinched as she twisted the ruler to tighten the makeshift tourniquet. The pain in my arm was excruciating and the tourniquet made it hurt even more. I shivered fitfully and closed my eyes, wishing I could escape the throng of schoolgirls and housewives gazing down at me. A woman in a flowery apron passed a cup of tea to Marina, who helped me sit up and held the cup to my lips. Tea—the great British cure-all for everything from heartbreak to machine-gun fire!

Gert squatted beside us and hissed, "Spies! Sympathizers! You nearly got what you deserve, didn't you?"

Pru gave Gert a stony glare. "Gert, shut up. If Sophie were a German spy, would the plane have taken aim at her? I don't think so, do you?"

"That's where you're wrong," Gert replied. "The Germans know we're on to Sophie and Marina—if that's their real names—and they want to get rid of them."

I sighed. I'd nearly had enough of Germans, of Gert, and of this whole stupid war.

Through gritted teeth, Marina said, "Well, if they know you're on to us, then someone must have told them, mustn't they? Oh, and who's the only person who 'knows' we're spies? Why, it's you, isn't it? So, who's in contact with the Germans? Doesn't take a rocket scientist to figure it out, does it?"

I wondered briefly if they even had rocket scientists in 1940.

"Good one, Marina," grinned Pru as Gert skulked off. "Oops, stand at attention, troops, here comes Miss Stanley."

"My goodness, what on earth happened? One of the girls said Sophie had been shot and killed."

Marina replied, "Shot, yes. Killed, no. Her arm is bleeding quite a lot though."

That was an understatement. The blood was seeping through the bandage Pru had contrived out of several handkerchiefs.

"Nice tourniquet, Prudence. Quick thinking. I've brought the first-aid kit, and an ambulance is on its way." Miss Stanley started to wind a new bandage on top of the makeshift one.

I winced. "Sorry, Miss Stanley, but it really does hurt quite a lot. Do you think the bullet's still in there?"

"No," Pru replied. "Only a flesh wound. It grazed you, actually. Took off a great lump of skin and stuff. Arm looks a bit like raw beef."

"Really, Prudence! Need you be so graphic? Oh, here's the ambulance at last."

Two women jumped out of the ambulance and cut through the crowd. "Well, it's not hard to see who got shot. How're you feeling, sweetie?"

"It hurts a lot. But I'm very lucky. Marina saved my life. I couldn't move. It's like I was hypnotized. I just looked at this plane coming at me, and it was shooting, and everyone else ran, but I was so stupid, I couldn't even move, and Marina could have been killed saving me, and it would have been all my fault!"

"Yes, but she wasn't, was she, so there's no point in thinking about 'what if.' Dear me, if we all sat around thinking 'what if' these days, where would we be? Come on, hop in the ambulance. Let's take you in."

"May I go, too, please?" Marina asked Miss Stanley. "I wouldn't be able to concentrate in school anyway."

Miss Stanley nodded. "Off you go, then. I'll telephone your guardian—Mr. Smith, isn't it?—and let him know to go to the hospital."

The ambulance driver helped me to my feet. Marina stooped and picked something up.

She grinned, holding up the bullet. "Souvenir! Quigs'll like that."

Pru climbed in the ambulance and gave me a hug. "Look after yourself, Sophie! Would Mrs. Quigley mind if I came around tonight to see you? Well, assuming there's no raid, I suppose. And that's a big assumption to make, eh?" She handed my crumpled, bloodstained raincoat and cardigan to Marina and jumped out. "Don't worry about Gert. I'll deal with her and put a stop to her shenanigans."

I wished she could, but I had a feeling Gert had not yet begun to fight.

》》》

The elderly doctor carefully unwound the bandages. "Right. Let's have a look at this arm of yours. Got winged, did you? Just as well Jerry's aim was a bit off. Dear me, how much have you got on here? Bandages, handkerchiefs, school ties—your friend certainly wasn't taking any chances, was she? Did quite a nice job of gift-wrapping you, actually. Let's have a look."

I bit my lip as he prodded my arm.

"Lots of fiber from your sweater in the wound. He almost missed you altogether. Another eighth of an inch, and you would have been fine. Mind you, another half an inch in the other direction, and you would have been in a very sorry state indeed. The nurse will clean the wound for you. You'll have quite a scar. Be something to show your grandchildren, though. They'll be interested to see what happened to Grandma in the war. We'll keep you in for a day or so and see how you get on. Might do a skin graft. Might not. Nurse! Take care of this young lady, please. Usual procedure."

The doctor pulled back the curtain and marched off. The nurse, a round-faced young woman with round glasses to match, came over from her post at the foot of the bed.

"Don't worry about the scar," the nurse said. "Maybe it'll heal all right. He's a bit of an old curmudgeon, but most of the young doctors have joined up. Shame, really. I only went into nursing to marry a doctor, and look at the choice I have."

Marina and I giggled.

"Hold on. This is going to hurt a bit. I'm going to have to make sure I get all the bits of wool and dirt out, otherwise you'll get a nasty infection."

Marina held my free hand tightly. I gasped as the nurse dabbed at my arm, but I was determined not to cry.

The curtain whisked back to reveal Mr. Schmidt, Esther, and a stern-looking woman wearing a dark blue dress and a frilly cap.

"Have you finished, Nurse?"

"Nearly, Sister."

The Sister came over and inspected my arm. She grunted, I assumed with approval, and nodded.

"This is Mr. Smith, the child's guardian. It appears her parents are deceased. And I believe you are acquainted with Esther Quigley." She glowered at Marina. "Now that Mr. Smith and Mrs. Quigley are here, you may join the boy in the waiting room. Carry on, Nurse."

The nurse squirted some kind of powder on my arm and started to apply another bandage.

"So, she's staying in overnight and is to be assessed tomorrow," Sister commented, looking at the chart on the bottom of the bed.

"Oh, can't she come home with us?" Esther asked.

"No, Mrs. Quigley, she cannot. As a nurse yourself, you should understand the importance of observation and particularly of cleanliness in the case of wounds such as this."

I looked up in surprise. I had no idea Esther was a nurse.

"Yes, Sister," Esther replied dutifully. Then, after the briefest of pauses, she said firmly but quietly, "No, Sister. My house is every bit as clean as this hospital, and I won't have you saying otherwise. I'm more than capable of observing a wound, and I'll bring her back tomorrow for the doctor to examine her. I would be much happier if, with all the bombings at night, I knew exactly where she was. My shelter's clean and watertight. Fred made absolutely sure of that. I know you never thought Fred was good enough to marry one of your precious nurses, but he took great pains to make sure ours was not going to be one of those shelters where you practically have to swim in and out. And, furthermore, while we're on the subject of Fred, I will have you know that every day and every night, he's up there," she stabbed her finger skyward, "making sure we're all safe. He's getting shot at and heaven knows what, and I won't have you say a word against anything he does."

From the look on the nurse's face, I don't think anyone had spoken to Sister like that before. Sister's expression softened.

"Mrs. Quigley, Esther, I am sure your house is wonderfully clean. You were an excellent nurse, and I can't imagine your standards slipped merely because you left the profession. I will have a word with Dr. Beedle, and see if he will discharge the girl to your care." With a starched swish, she left the cubicle.

"Blimey, Esther, you were fantastic," the staff nurse whispered. "I don't think anyone's ever disagreed with Sister."

"Well, they have now. Slip us a couple of dressings and bandages, would you? Cheers." Esther carefully wrapped the bandages in a clean hankie and stowed them in her handbag.

Sister crackled back. "Dr. Beedle says because it's you, and only because it's you, you may take Sophie back home. He always had a soft spot for you; we all did. But she must be here at ten o'clock tomorrow morning sharp to have her wound inspected and to be assessed for further treatment."

"Yes, Sister. Thank you, Sister."

Sister turned her keen eyes on me. "And you, young lady, are truly fortunate indeed to be living with a nurse of the caliber of Mrs. Quigley. You will do everything she says and you will not, repeat not, play outside until that arm is well and truly healed. Oh, and stay out the way of low-flying aircraft in the future, would you? We have quite enough to do with people who don't see the bomb coming to deal with those who stand there and let someone take aim at them." A quick smile took the sting from the words. She nodded in Esther's direction and rustled out.

"There! All done!" The nurse finished her handiwork and patted my shoulder. "Jump down. It was lovely to see you again, Esther. We still miss you after five years. You always were the only person who could handle Sister."

Esther gave the nurse a quick hug. I took the opportunity to escape to the waiting room. Quigs jumped up.

"Are you okay, Soph? When the Head came in and told Henry you'd been shot, I thought he meant shot dead. Not just hit in the arm."

"Don't look so disappointed," I teased. "Although I could have been dead if Marina hadn't knocked me flying. I was standing there like an idiot and she tackled me from behind. Don't know what hurt worse—the bullet or having the air knocked out of me!"

"Well, anyway, I'm glad you're not dead. But don't tell anyone else I said that. Marina showed me your bullet; you don't want it, do you? Can I have it? It'll be the star piece of my collection. Well, until I get a German helmet or a machine gun or something, anyway."

Mr. Schmidt's voice came from behind. "Well, that isn't likely, I hope, so you will have to make do with the bullet. I think you have been remarkably brave, Sophie. Although if you did this merely to get out of school lunch, I shall be very cross indeed. We'll take a taxi home, in case someone bangs Sophie's arm on the bus. Esther's just gone to call for one."

I told Mr. Schmidt and Quigs about Gert's latest accusations. Mr. Schmidt sighed heavily.

"She could be extremely dangerous. Perhaps she would change if you girls befriended her. Very often, bullies are simply lonely and frightened. Maybe she has a troubled home life."

"If she doesn't, she certainly deserves one," I retorted. I blushed as Mr. Schmidt looked reprovingly at me. "No, honestly, sir, it would be like befriending a snake. You'd never know when she was going to bite you or choke you or something."

"Well, if you can't stay out of her way, and you won't befriend her, we are running out of options, aren't we? Ah, Esther is beckoning us; the taxi must be here. If Quigs and I go straight to school, we will be back in good time for lunch. And Marina, I think you may as well go back to school as well. Miss Stanley will be anxiously awaiting a report on Sophie, as will your friends."

"As will Gert," muttered Marina, climbing into the taxi.

I met her eyes. Maybe Mr. Schmidt was right. Maybe we should try to befriend Gert. What harm could it do?

❱❱❱

"Hello, Sophie, old pal!" Pru greeted me from the kitchen doorway. "Well, I suppose getting shot is one way of getting out of doing the dishes. Hello, Mrs. Quigley. I'm Prudence Makepeace. I hope you don't mind me barging into your kitchen; that gorgeous Mr. Smith let me in."

"Pleased to meet you, Pru! Of course I don't mind; I've heard so much about you."

"Oh, dear, that's what everyone says," Pru said, smiling. "Actually, I come bearing gifts. Well, not gifts as such, but I hope they'll be useful. Sophie rather ruined her coat and sweater today—"

"Hey! It wasn't my fault. Well, not entirely," I protested.

"—and so my mother sent me around with one of my coats I've grown out of and a couple of sweaters. They're in good shape, I think you'll find. I hope you'll take them, otherwise my mother will feel guilty about having perfectly good clothes hanging around the house, and may start chopping bits off me so that I'll fit into them again."

Esther dried her hands on her apron and held up the coat. "Why, this is perfect. It's like brand-new. You must have been really well-behaved to have kept your clothes in such wonderful condition."

Pru hooted with laughter. "I'd like to be able to agree, but the only reason that coat is like it is, is that we bought it on sale at the beginning of the summer three years ago, and then I had a growth spurt, and was too big for it before I had a chance to wear it. Mum was not pleased and got me a second-hand one instead. Still, it was her fault for feeding me so well. Now, Sophie, how's your arm? Wow, that's an impressive-looking bandage. And a sling, too!"

"Esther put the sling on because my arm hurts less when it's not hanging down. I don't think I said thank you for looking after me, did I?"

"Oh, think nothing of it. As a little girl, I always bandaged up my dolls, dogs, and cats. In fact, once I bandaged up my little brother so effectively that he stomped around like an Egyptian mummy for hours until my mother made me unwrap him. Hello, who's this coming to your back door? If it's not Herbert Martin! I haven't seen him in years, thank heaven. Not since we started secondary school."

Marina opened the back door. "Hello, Bert! Have you come to see our celebrity?"

Bert's cold eyes flicked over me. "Actually, no. Although my mum did send these blackberry tarts for her. Mr. Smith said he'd help me with my French." He handed a cloth-covered plate to Esther.

"He's in the sitting room, Bert. Go on in."

"Strange, strange boy," Pru commented. "Always struck me as odd."

I tried to sound nonchalant. "Why?"

"He was in my brother's class and Ted—that's my brother—said Bert simply refused to study history. 'Don't worry about the past,' he kept telling the teacher. Got in loads of trouble for his attitude. But on the other hand, he refused to say what he wanted to be when he grew up. Most boys say they want to be a fireman or a train driver, but not Bert, oh no. All he would say is 'Don't worry about the future.' Decidedly odd. Maybe someone dropped a clock on his head at birth." She shrugged. "Still, enough of strange boys! I must get going before some strange German boy drops a bomb between here and my house. I also have some French homework to do. Say, I don't suppose your lovely Mr. Smith would give me a hand? But no, maybe not; my mind definitely wouldn't be on verbs." With a dramatic sigh and swoon, she stood up. I followed her to the front door.

"Goodnight, chaps!" Pru said as she passed in front of the sitting room.

Mr. Schmidt stood up. "Goodnight, Prudence. Thank you so much for looking after Sophie today. We are all in your debt." He shook Pru's hand. "And can you tell me please, what you know of this girl called Gert?"

"A nasty piece of work. She's the youngest of four children. Mother runs a rooming house. The whole family squeezes into two rooms to make more space for the boarders. They don't have two coins to rub together. My mother says Gert's dad sloped off when she was little, and she says knowing what Gert's mother is like, it's little wonder. Evidently, Gert inherited her charm from her mum."

"Youngest of four children, hmmm? Does she have any brothers in school? I wonder if I teach any of them."

"Well, she would have one in Fourth Form; though I doubt he spends much time in school. Never did in primary. But maybe I'm wrong. His name is Joshua Pratt."

CHAPTER 8

⟫⟫⟫ Friday, September 20, 1940

For the second time in five days—five days! Was that how long it had been here?—Esther woke me up with tea and toast. She threw open the curtains.

"Good morning, patient! And how did we sleep last night?"

"Well, I don't know about you, but I think I got about five minutes after we got back to bed. Those bombs were incredibly close last night. Where did they hit? Do you know?"

"Just a few streets over. The other boys' school had loads of its windows blown out, Bob next door told Quigs this morning. Quigs is really jealous because Bob has a day off from school, and he doesn't. Still, he'll have all next week off, won't he?"

I climbed out of bed and looked out of the window at the plumes of smoke curling gracefully skyward from the bombed houses. Across the tracks, children lined up in their class groups as a teacher swung her brass hand bell.

"My goodness, is it that late? Has Marina gone to school?"

"Yes, Pru came to get her about a half an hour ago. Eat your toast and wash your face. I'll change your dressing and then it'll be time to go to the hospital for your appointment."

"I won't have to have a skin graft, will I? How do they do that?"

"Oh, I'll spare you the gory details, but basically, the surgeon takes a portion of skin from your thigh, and sews it on to your arm.

Maybe Dr. Beedle won't think it's necessary. In times like these, I'm sure they have enough people to operate on."

I grimaced at the thought and bit into my toast. Mmmm, Marmite, my favorite, lovely spread. "So why didn't Sister like you marrying Fred? If I'm not being too nosy."

"Sister didn't like any of her nurses leaving the profession, well, except for those who she thought were too flighty to be a nurse. But, if we had to marry, it had better be to a "professional" person—a doctor would be good, although heaven help us if she ever caught us even talking to one!—or a lawyer, something fancy or posh. Fred, you see, is not posh. He came from a good family, but he didn't quite fit the bill. His grandma left him this house when she died. He could never have hoped to buy anything like this on his own. Anyway, he used to race motorcycles at Crystal Palace Park. He fell off his bike and they took him to the hospital to be patched up, and that's where I met him."

"Oh, so you were his nurse!"

"That's right." Esther gazed dreamily out the window. "Love at first sight. I had to wash the blood out of his lovely red hair, and get the grease and dirt out of his skin where he'd skidded along the ground. He broke his right wrist and his left leg. Dear me, he was a mess. But those eyes, and that smile—" She broke off. Her voice became matter-of-fact. "Sister said he'd never amount to anything, that I'd be sorry if I married him. Well, he did amount to something, didn't he, and I'll never be sorry for marrying him. Never, never, never!"

I leaped out of bed and gave Esther a tight hug with my good arm. Oh, how I wished I could change Esther's future for her. It was so unfair. War sucks.

"Right, madam, enough of this. Get yourself ready in the bathroom and then come downstairs to the kitchen and we'll dress your wound. Dr. Beedle is not going to see that arm looking anything other than its best."

❱❱❱

I held Esther's hand in the hospital waiting room, terrified of what Dr. Beedle would say. My arm had bled during the night and the bandage had stuck to the raw wound. Even though Esther was as gentle as she could, the pain had been agonizing when she'd removed the bandage. Joseph had been fascinated by the procedure until I'd started to cry, which started him bawling.

A tall, thin nurse ushered us into Dr. Beedle's tiny office.

"Miss Pinkerton. Nurse Paterson." Dr. Beedle looked up from his notes and surveyed us over the tops of his little half-moon glasses.

"Quigley," Esther corrected him firmly. "It's Esther Quigley now."

"Right. Okay, young lady, let's see how that arm's doing. Managed to avoid the Luftwaffe last night, did you?" He unwrapped Esther's handiwork. "Hmmm, satisfactory healing thus far. No immediate signs of infection." I flinched as he touched the wound. "Nurse, observations?"

"Some bleeding overnight, which is to be expected. Blood only, no pus. Good mobility to the fingers. Strong pulse. Normal temperature. Aside from the obvious pain, the patient seems all right."

"Good. Good. Well, I don't think we need to bother with a skin graft. I have plenty of other patients who need my time and skills more than this young lady does. Nurse, pop another bandage on, and you may take her home."

Esther busied herself with the bandages while Dr. Beedle scribbled on the chart.

"Sister tells me your husband is in the Air Force. He does like machines that go fast, doesn't he? I was in the cavalry in World War I. Give me a horse over one of those airplanes any day. I believe you were expecting a baby when you left the hospital. Is this young man the result?"

"Yes, doctor. Joseph is four now, and I have another on the way."

He fished around in his desk drawer. "I think I have—oh yes, here it is! Look, Joseph! Would you like a chocolate?"

Joseph's eyes grew big and round. Candy was in very short supply. He looked up at Esther.

"Yes, you may, Joseph. Say thank you to Dr. Beedle."

Joseph chanted his thanks, took the chocolate and handed it to Esther to unwrap. She popped it in his mouth.

Dr. Beedle shook his head sadly. "What a world for children to grow up in. Their first impressions are hatred, fear, and death. Not good. Not good at all." He paused and fiddled with his pen. "I—I heard last week my son was killed at sea. He was a doctor in the Navy."

"Oh, Dr. Beedle! I'm so terribly sorry." Esther's head jerked up, her eyes filling with tears.

The elderly doctor sighed. "I hope your husband comes home soon and your children are raised in a better world than this. Get yourself off now, and tell that old trout of a nurse out there to send in the next victim."

❱❱❱

Esther, Joseph and I spent a pleasant afternoon picking the last of the blackberries from the bushes beside the railroad tracks. Clouds raced across the sky, letting the pale sun peek anemically through from time to time. The sounds of children laughing and playing wafted over from the school on the other side of the tracks. A blackbird sang sweetly from a rooftop. We could pretend the world was at peace until the buzz of engines overhead shattered the idyll. Esther and I gazed skyward, shielding our eyes with our hands.

"Ours," Esther pronounced.

"Is it Daddy? Is it Daddy?" Joseph jumped up and down, pulling at Esther's dress.

"Could be, Joseph. Let's give them a wave, just in case."

We flailed our arms like windmills until the planes disappeared from sight.

"The baby's due five months from today. Well, more or less." Esther rubbed her tummy. "I wonder if the war will be over by then. I want my baby to be born surrounded by peace and happiness, not born in a rotten Anderson shelter with bombs exploding all around. Dr. Beedle was right; what sort of a start in life is that? I want to be able to put the baby outside in his pram, and not to have to wonder if he's going to get blown to bits or shot. Stupid, stupid, stupid war!"

"Do you know if Fred is going to get any leave soon?"

"No. All his leave has been cancelled. Can't have the men doing happy things like finding out their wives are pregnant in the middle of a war, can we? Dear me, no. But I did write to him to tell him I had you staying with me. I think he'll be glad of that. He worries about me being by myself, and would rather I went to the country to my aunt's or even moved in with my sister and her brood. I didn't tell him how handsome Henry is; I don't want him to get the wrong idea. I just said he teaches at the boys' school. He'll probably imagine Henry to be somewhat dusty, gray and thin, with little wire spectacles."

We shrieked with laughter, and linking arms, went in to make an apple and blackberry pie for tea.

❱ ❱ ❱

Esther was upstairs with Joseph and I was busy washing the blackberries, making sure there were no little wigglies in them when Marina came home. She listened while I told her about our trip to the hospital, and then jumped up and took a paper bag out of her satchel.

"Look what the girls did in domestic science for you. No, it's not a pair of army socks." She handed me the bag.

"It doesn't explode, does it? No, I suppose that would have been from the girls in regular science." I peeked in the bag and took out a cream tray cloth, embroidered with all the girls' names.

"Yesterday and today, the girls took turns embroidering their names on the cloth for you. The teacher hemmed it."

Tears stung my eyes as I examined the cloth closely. I couldn't believe the girls I had known for only a few days would have taken the time to do this for me. Some of the stitching wasn't very neat, and there was a small dot of blood where a finger had been pricked, but it was one of the nicest things I had ever been given. I smoothed it carefully on the kitchen table.

"I'm glad Gert isn't in our class. She probably would have put a swastika on it."

"I tried to talk to her today, like Henry suggested. Didn't get very far. She accused me of trying to infiltrate the locals. What a hoot! I wonder if she's a relative of Miss Pratt. Maybe a great-aunt or something."

"But Miss Pratt's so posh. I can't imagine her ever being related to someone like Gert."

"Well, people do manage to turn their lives around. I'm sure Miss Pratt's first name is Trudy."

"So?"

"Oh, Sophie! What's Gert short for? Gertrude. Gertrude—Trudy. Don't you see? How much of a coincidence would that be? I think Miss Pratt must have been named after Gert. Maybe Gertrude is a family name, but Miss Pratt's mother thought it was simply too awful to call her baby, so she made it Trudy."

I went back to the sink and continued washing the blackberries.

"So, Marina, how old do you think Miss Pratt is?"

Marina thought for a minute. "I don't know. It's hard to say. I've heard her talk about retiring, so she must be getting up there. Let's say she's in her late fifties. And Gert is about thirteen." I could see the well-oiled wheels in Marina's head turning. She clapped her hand over her mouth. "I wonder if Gert is actually Miss Pratt's mother!"

We gaped at each other.

"But when Gert got married, she wouldn't have been a Pratt any more."

"No, unless she didn't get married. Dear me, can you imagine anyone actually marrying Gert?"

I shook my head. I still couldn't connect the vile, coarse Gert Pratt with our elegant head teacher. An idea struck me.

"I know! Tomorrow, let's go and find out where Gert lives. If she sees us, well, we can say we're on our way somewhere else. Anyway, wouldn't you like to see what that bit of Penge was like during the war? We've only seen the nice places."

"Okay. But I hope we don't run into Gert, or she really will think we're spying."

I laughed. "And for once, she would be right."

CHAPTER 9

⟩⟩⟩ Saturday, September 21, 1940

I sat quietly at the breakfast table while Esther inspected my arm. It still oozed a little bit but Esther was pleased with my progress. I was relieved she thought I wouldn't have much of a scar, merely a pockmark or two. I couldn't imagine how I would explain anything worse to my mother when I got back to my own time—if I got back. However, while I was in 1940, I might as well enjoy myself as much as possible.

"Esther, would it be all right if I went out for a walk with Marina today? After I've helped you with the housework, of course."

"I don't see why not. Planning on going into Penge? Going to the pictures, maybe?"

"Maybe. Or just to look at the shops. I don't know, really."

Mr. Schmidt looked at me over the top of the *Beckenham Journal.* I blushed. He could always tell if someone was being less than honest. He knew I was up to something.

Esther looked at him and then at me. Oh dear, she'd obviously figured out I was fibbing. Sometimes it's much easier to tell the truth, particularly if you are not a good liar. She left the room, leaving me alone with Mr. Schmidt.

Mr. Schmidt laid down his newspaper.

"Sophie, what are you and Marina planning? You are not going to the pictures at all, are you?"

"I—um—might be."

"Oh, Sophie, don't bother lying. You don't do it at all well. Now, what are you up to?"

"It's nothing, really. We only want to see where Gert lives. That's all."

"And why the sudden interest in someone you have been trying to avoid all week? I would have thought you would have gone in the opposite direction. Or are you taking my advice and befriending her?" He examined my face shrewdly through narrowed eyes. "No, I see that isn't it. Is it because of her last name? Ah ha! I thought so!"

I drew in my breath defensively. "Well, Marina and I want to see where Gert lives because we figured out she must be Miss Pratt's mother."

"Oh, you did, did you? And how did you reach this conclusion?"

"Because of the names. Miss Pratt's first name is Trudy, isn't it, and Gertrude is so similar to Trudy, and they are the right sort of ages to be mother and daughter."

Mr. Schmidt spoke very softly. "And so what if they are mother and daughter? What if Miss Pratt does manage to free herself from the grinding poverty in which Gert Pratt obviously lives, according to Pru? So what? Is it any business of yours?"

I felt myself shrinking to about two inches high. I wished someone would come in and rescue me from this cross-examination.

"Think of this from Gert's standpoint. You supposedly come from the East End. If that is the case, then you should be as poor as she is. But no, here you are living in a fine house with nice clothes. And then Gert looks out of her window and sees you and Marina staring at her house. How is she to feel? Is this going to make her feel kindly towards you? No! And rightly so. You would be looking at her and the way she is forced to live like you would look at an animal in a zoo. Maybe not unkindly, but with the same sort of detached, superior attitude."

That was too much. How could Mr. Schmidt think that of me?

"No! I don't feel superior at all. Remember, I live in a basement flat. Marina's father hasn't had a job in years. We're not rich, so why would we be looking down on Gert?"

Mr. Schmidt's face softened. He nodded slowly. "I know, Sophie, you and Marina are kind girls. You would not deliberately hurt anyone. But be careful of other people's feelings and think about the impression they might get from your actions. It would appear to Gert, at least, that you were gloating over the difference in your circumstances. But since you are determined to know about Miss Pratt, I shall tell you. This information will not reach the twenty-first century. Is that clear?" I nodded.

"I, too, believe Gert Pratt is Miss Pratt's mother. Miss Pratt has told me she came from a poor background, but she was determined to pull herself out of it and to help other people. She realized the best way she could do this would be to become a teacher and to help mold other children who might be in similar circumstances. I don't know all the details, of course, but I do know that her mother—Gert—worked her fingers to the bone to keep her daughter in school. Ha! That surprised you, didn't it? You may have noticed how Miss Pratt shows a special interest in disadvantaged children. That is directly because of her background. She knows it is sometimes difficult for them to stay in school and to beat the cycle of poverty, and she does everything in her power to help them. So, now you know." He leaned back in his chair, his eyes probing my face. "What are you going to do with that information, Sophie Pinkerton?"

I fiddled with my spoon. The fact that Gert had managed to produce Miss Pratt still staggered me, and it must have been even harder to have been a single parent in the nineteen forties than it was in the twenty-first century. Gert had struggled to make sure her daughter's life would be better than her own. A wave of dismay at the thought of the road ahead for Gert washed over me. I wished I didn't know what was to happen. This knowledge of the future was becoming a terribly heavy burden.

"I'm sorry, sir," I whispered. "You're right. I didn't think."

Mr. Schmidt rewarded me with one of his wonderful smiles. "That's okay, Sophie. You're thinking now; that's the main thing. Tell you what! Let's go to the pictures this afternoon, all six of us. I believe that in the nineteen forties you got a cartoon, a newsreel, two features—we can spend the afternoon forgetting about the war. Well, except for during the newsreel, that is."

I brightened and jumped up. "Brilliant! I'll go and tell the others." I ran around the table and planted a kiss on Mr. Schmidt's cheek.

Open up, floor. Open up now and swallow me.
But the floor didn't open, so I fled.

》 》 》

One thing about 1940, there were plenty of theaters. Penge seemed to have three, from what I saw in the newspaper. The Odeon was right across the road from the school so we didn't have far to walk.

A blue fog of cigarette smoke hung low over the auditorium. I was going to smell like an old chimney by the time the movie ended. Marina pinched my arm as we slid over to our seats and nodded down towards the front of the theater. Oh, wonderful. Gert. Hopefully, she wouldn't see us. I was glad when the houselights dimmed and "God Save the King" started.

I had gone an entire week without television. Surprisingly, I wasn't going into withdrawal, probably because there were so many new experiences to occupy my mind. Having bombs dropped on you and being shot certainly gives you something new to think about. Nevertheless, I was excited when the heavy velvet curtains opened and the Pathé newsreel began. The horrors of war flashed before my eyes. It had been easy to watch old news clips in history class, but now they were more sinister, more real. I was no longer sitting in my comfortable, safe classroom, watching the war from a distance; now it was happening to me. Any one of those Spitfires on the film could be piloted by Fred. Any of the Messerschmitts that flew past the camera's lens could have been the one that shot me. And any of the people shown standing by the smoking wrecks of their houses could be someone sitting in this theater.

I was relieved when the newsreel ended and the cartoon began. We all laughed uproariously through the cartoon and the comedy feature—probably much more than we would have without the relief of forgetting about the war for a few hours. As the houselights went up, I noticed Gert had turned around in her seat and was staring straight at me. I hoped I could leave before she had a chance to spoil this lovely afternoon.

"Come on!" I whispered to Marina. We cut through the crowd as quickly as we could. But we weren't quick enough. I yelped as a hand grabbed my arm, gripping my wound cruelly.

"Let her go!" Marina cried, swinging her gas mask at Gert.

An usher hurried up. "Is there a problem here, girls?'

From behind me, Mr. Schmidt said, "It's all right. I will take care of this. Well, girls, would you like to introduce me to this young lady?"

Gert gaped at Mr. Schmidt, dropping my arm. I rubbed it, determined not to cry.

I was glad to see Esther approaching with a sleepy-looking Joseph in tow.

"Hello, Gert! How are you doing? I was talking to your mother in the butcher's yesterday. She didn't look very well, poor thing."

"Probably drunk," Gert muttered under her breath. Louder, she said: "She's all right, Mrs. Quigley. Look, I have to go. Mum's expecting me."

She pushed past, giving Mr. Schmidt a frightened glance and shooting Marina and me a look of pure venom.

Esther sighed. "Poor thing. She doesn't have much of a life. She's only able to come to the theater because one of her brothers runs the projector, and he gets her in for free. Only bit of pleasure she gets. Her mother's generally drunk as a lord, so the chore of looking after her brothers and that boarding house falls on Gert. There ought to be a law against it."

Mr. Schmidt picked up Joseph and put him on his shoulders. "Have you known her family long?"

"Oh, yes. I went to school for a while with Gert's aunt. The whole family has always been a bad bunch. I fear for that girl, though, I really do. With all the other troubles in the world, people like Gert get lost in the shuffle. And with some of the characters who frequent that boarding house—" She broke off, shaking her head.

Marina and I looked at each other. It was no wonder Gert was unpleasant. How easy it was to take people at face value, without thinking about what made them tick. How easy, and how wrong.

Nevertheless, I was stunned to hear Marina say: "Is there anything we can do to help her?"

Esther sighed deeply. "Who knows? It would probably be a bit like trying to help a wild animal with its leg caught in a trap. You might free it in time, but you'd be bitten in the process. Oh, look!

There's Bert Martin. Quigs, why don't you run over and ask if he'd like to come around after tea? You've spent all afternoon with adults and two girls. You deserve some young male companionship."

"All right! Thanks, Esther!" Quigs took off.

"I know what! Let's have a little party tonight to celebrate—oh, what can we celebrate? So much sadness and gloom. Well, we can celebrate that at least we have each other and we're alive. Oh dear, was that insensitive because of your parents?" She looked worried.

Marina squeezed her arm. "No, of course not. We're not the only people who've lost our families. And like you said, at least we have each other. No use being miserable. Time enough for that."

I caught Marina's eye. I knew we were both thinking the same thing. There would be time enough to be miserable when someone really had died. And that would be soon enough.

)))

Marina and I sat cross-legged on Esther's bed while Esther rummaged through a huge trunk, pulling out party dresses from happier times.

"Ah! This is what I was looking for! I wore this the day I got engaged to Fred. It would probably fit you best, Marina, since you're taller than Sophie and a little more—filled out, shall we say." Esther held up a beautiful dress with short sleeves, tiny pleats down the bodice and about six yards of material in the skirt. "It's horribly wrinkled, but we can soon fix that with the iron."

She passed it to Marina who danced around the bedroom, clutching the dress in front of her.

"Oh, Esther! It's just beautiful! Are you sure you want me to wear it? I mean, it's such a special dress. I'd be terrified of spilling something on it."

"Not much danger of that; we don't have a lot of food to spill. It's a bit big, isn't it? Never mind, we'll take it in. Won't take long. Now, Sophie. I know I've just the thing for you in here." Esther's head and half her body disappeared into the trunk. "Ta-daaaa! Here we are. This was my first 'grown-up' dress. I got it for my uncle's wedding in—oh my goodness—1925, I think. I'm glad I never throw anything out."

I gasped as Esther produced the most gorgeous dress I have ever seen. It was made of shimmery chiffon, which changed color as the light hit it. The waistline was low, right on the hips, and the skirt flared out to the knee. The dress had a shawl collar, just covering the shoulders.

I touched the fabric gently. "Oh, Esther! I've never worn anything like this before."

"Well," Esther said firmly, "there's a first time for everything. And if we're going to have a party, then we have to dress for the occasion. We'll show those men what gorgeous women we are. Now, as for me—" She frowned and pulled her dress tight to show her expanding tummy. "Well, I suppose for me, it's my one party frock from when I was pregnant with Joseph." From the back of her wardrobe she brought out a dark red velvet dress. "There! That won't look too shabby, will it? Sophie, you run down to the kitchen and get the iron and the ironing board, and we'll start our alterations."

I bounced down the stairs and into the kitchen. I stopped short in amazement at the sight of Mr. Schmidt wearing Esther's apron, rolling out pastry.

"Ah! Bet you didn't know I could cook, did you? My talents are many and varied. I thought I would make one or two things—a few sausage rolls and little tarts. Esther was going to cook the sausages for tea, so I thought why not make them into sausage rolls? It is my contribution to the party. Quigs and Bert have gone to get some gramophone records from Bert's aunt. Evidently, she has all the latest music from North America as she is seeing a Canadian soldier. So, this should be good fun tonight, *ja?*"

I longed to tell Mr. Schmidt about my beautiful dress, but a cloying mass of infantile shyness smothered the words. Head down to conceal my burning cheeks, I ducked into the cupboard and picked up the ironing board and the iron.

"Oh, and Sophie," Mr. Schmidt called after me as I escaped as quickly as I could with my unwieldy load, "if you ever tell anyone you have seen me in a frilly apron—"

"I know, I know! I'll have detention for the rest of my life."

〉〉〉

"Let's have one more look at you." Esther tied a long silk scarf over my bandage, leaving the ends floating loose. "Hmm, that's not bad. Not bad at all."

I surveyed our reflections in the mirror. "Not bad" was the understatement of the year. Even I looked—well, could I really say I looked pretty? Would that be bragging? I sighed. I certainly felt pretty. Esther had even found shoes for Marina and me. Our feet seemed to be quite a bit wider than hers, but we certainly couldn't wear our normal clunky school shoes with our beautiful dresses.

I pushed Marina toward the door. I had no intention of going downstairs first, and I didn't want to follow Esther in case I clumsily tripped and knocked her down the stairs.

Joseph was waiting at the bottom of the stairs. "Mummy's coming!" he shouted. "Mummy!"

Mr. Schmidt, Quigs, and Bert came out of the sitting room. Bert gave a long wolf whistle. I blushed fiercely.

"Whoa! You look great!" Quigs said, his eyes wide. "Considering that you're Soph and Marina, that is."

I couldn't bear to look at Mr. Schmidt. Oh, how I wished I were ten years older. Or even seven or eight years older. Just older would do.

"You are beautiful, ladies," Mr. Schmidt said. "All of you. We are extremely honored to be in your presence."

He stood aside so we could enter the sitting room.

Esther gasped as she saw the food on the table. "My, Henry, where did all this come from?"

"Oh, I made one or two things. Don't worry; the boys helped me clean up the kitchen. And Quigs says to tell you he made the sandwiches."

"Corned beef," Quigs announced proudly. "Well, a tiny bit of corned beef. Mostly bread and margarine. And Henry made the sausage rolls and things. Oh, come on. We've stared at you, you've stared at the table. Now can't we eat before the air raid starts?"

We laughed and dug in. Bert put a record on the gramophone. Esther jumped up as big-band music filled the room.

"Roll up the carpet, boys. Let's dance! Oh, I haven't danced in ages and ages. Not since Fred was last home."

Mr. Schmidt and the boys shoved the furniture out of the way and slid the carpet to the side of the room. Esther gracefully swayed over to the gramophone, munching on a sandwich as she went.

"Let's see what you have. Oh! Glenn Miller's new one—'In the Mood.' Well, I'm certainly in the mood." She placed the record on the gramophone. "Come on, Henry." She grabbed his hand and pulled him to the center of the room, tapping her feet to the beat.

"But your condition. Should you dance to such a fast song?"

"With Joseph, I danced until I was in my eighth month. Makes for an easier birth. Come on!"

In an instant, they were whirling and twirling. He spun her around and around, backwards and forwards, side to side. My feet wouldn't keep still. I was itching to join in.

"Come on Marina!" Bert cried, dragging her to her feet.

"I've never—"

"Oh, it's easy. Come on, you two. Don't just sit there."

I'd never danced like this before. Oh, be honest. I'd never danced at all before. I never even knew I could; and I certainly didn't dream Quigs could dance. But here we were, jitterbugging—maybe not with Mr. Schmidt's and Esther's expertise, but jitterbugging, nevertheless.

"Oh!" Esther gasped, hanging onto Mr. Schmidt's arm as the record finished. "Oh dear, I'm out of breath." She collapsed on the couch and fanned herself with her hand. "Sophie and Marina, go into the pantry and on the top shelf you'll find a bottle, towards the back. It's raspberry cordial I made last summer. Can you bring it in with a pitcher of water? Thanks."

Marina opened the pantry door and turned on the light.

"The blackout!" I gasped.

She hastily turned off the light and shut the door behind us, plunging us into darkness. Giggling, I felt my way, reached up and pulled down the blind over the small, high window. At that same moment, the air-raid siren started to wail.

"Oh no! Well, so much for our party."

Esther appeared in the doorway. "Grab the cordial anyway. We'll simply move the party out to the shelter. There won't be room to dance, but we can still have fun. Now, hurry! Quigs, there's an old wind-up gramophone in the front parlor, can you carry it? It's quite heavy. Bert, bring what food you can and the gramophone records. Use that cardboard box there; that way you can carry more. Henry's getting Joseph. Girls, don't forget your coats and change your shoes."

"Too bad we didn't plan this in advance," Esther said as we giggled our way into the shelter. "We could have hung some paper chains from the ceiling. Still, never mind. We have music and food and raspberry cordial; what more do we need?"

Quigs balanced the gramophone carefully on one of the chairs, and Marina arranged the plates of food on the bookcase. With a flourish, Esther produced six beautiful crystal glasses, which she had carefully wrapped in a tea towel.

"Henry, if you can pour the cordial, please. Only fill the glasses half-full; it needs to be diluted."

Bert topped up the glasses from the shelter's water bottle, which Esther filled with fresh water every day.

Esther's eyes widened as she took a sip.

"Oh, my goodness!" she laughed. "It's fermented since last year and turned alcoholic. Plain water for Joseph, I think. And we'd better water down the children's a bit more."

Marina, Quigs, Bert and I took long gulps before Esther had a chance to grab our glasses.

Bert rolled his eyes. "Wow, Mrs. Quigley, if you ever need to make money quick, you could open a still. This is great!"

Mr. Schmidt went into Instant Teacher Mode. "Children, your glasses, please. Bert, I am not returning you to your mother rolling drunk. Give it here."

I took another sip and grinned at Mr. Schmidt wickedly over the top of my glass.

"Oh, but sir, this is full of vitamin C. Just what we need to stay healthy in wartime. And it keeps our spirits up, too. I'm sure if Mr. Churchill tasted some of this, he'd have the Ministry of Food put it in the ration books, and make Esther Minister of Raspberry Cordial!" I was starting to feel quite giggly and light headed.

Esther chuckled. "Oh, Henry, will one glass really do them so much harm? This war has torn their childhoods away. If they have to be grown up before their time, let them at least have a glass of wine. Mr. and Mrs. Martin won't care, I can promise you that. I went to school with Vera Martin, and I can definitely assure you she won't mind!" Esther dissolved in a fit of giggles. "Somebody wind up that gramophone. What shall we have? 'Tuxedo Junction?' Come on, Quigs, put it on for us. Let Jerry do his worst up there, he can't spoil our fun in here!"

CHAPTER 10

⟫⟫ Sunday, September 22, 1940

I sat up in bed, groaning.

"Oh, Marina! My head hurts. Oh dear, I don't feel well at all."

Marina opened one rather bloodshot eye.

"I think the cordial was even stronger than we thought. Oooh, if this is a hangover, I am never, never, never getting tipsy again."

She moaned and pulled her pillow over her head.

I crawled out of bed and into my robe. Maybe if I washed my face and brushed my teeth I would feel human again.

"Good morning, Sophie!" called Mr. Schmidt cheerily, as he came out of his room. "How are you this morning? Full of the joys of spring? Glad to hear it!" He slapped me on the back, and hurried down the stairs, laughing loudly.

"Shuddup," I muttered at his hastily departing back.

Oh no. Esther and Joseph were coming out of Joseph's room. This landing was getting more and more like Paddington Station every second.

"Dear me!" Esther tutted. "Rather the worse for wear, are we?"

They bounced downstairs singing "Run Rabbit Run" at the top of their lungs. Why did everyone have to be so perky today?

I took refuge in the bathroom. Ugh, was that person in the mirror really me? My hair stuck out at odd angles from my head. My eyelids were swollen and red. I poked out my tongue. It was covered with white scum. Gross. And people got drunk for fun? I'd only had a little, and I looked and felt like death warmed over.

I splashed cold water on my face and brushed my teeth and tongue with the nasty scrubbing brush that passed for a toothbrush in 1940. I dragged a comb through my tangled mop and slicked it down with water. Well, I supposed I looked a bit more like a human being. I gazed longingly at the bath, with its required-by-the-war-effort five-inch water level marked sternly in black around the inside. What I wouldn't give for a long, deep soak. Never mind.

I opened the bathroom door to find Quigs waiting outside, his fist raised, ready to pound on the door. We both gasped in horror—me at nearly having my face pounded instead of the door, and Quigs, well, because he's Quigs.

"Good grief, Soph! I've seen some frightening sights since we've been here, but you take the cake. We could send you to Germany as Britain's Secret Weapon. Scare Hitler into submission."

"Quigs, shut up and move before I throw up on your feet. Because that is how I feel."

Quigs shut up and moved.

I staggered downstairs and into the kitchen. I was glad to see the weather was in sympathy with me. A thick gray fog blanketed the garden, just like the thick gray fog that blanketed my brain.

Esther smiled kindly over the top of her teacup. "Dry toast, aspirin, and black tea for you, I think. I feel so awful about that cordial. If I'd had any idea it had become so incredibly alcoholic, I'd never had served it. Not to you children, anyway! So, what are you up to today?"

"Not a lot. Are there any chores you need us to do?" I offered.

"You can dust, if you like. And the air-raid shelter needs a good cleaning. I hope you won't think I'm rude, but Joseph and I go to Cora's—that's my sister—every Sunday for dinner. I wish I could invite you, but—"

"Esther! We wouldn't dream of imposing," Mr. Schmidt protested. "I think the children and I are more than capable of looking after ourselves. You must go to your sister's, stay as long as you like, and have a lovely time. If you want to stay late, I would be happy to come and escort you home."

"Oh, that's sweet. But she only lives across the road from the school; it's not far at all. I'll leave the address on the table in case there's an emergency. Well, good morning, Quigs! You look like you're in better shape than Sophie. Have you two seen anything of Marina this morning?"

"I last saw her with her head stuffed under a pillow," I replied. "Her face was about the same color as her eyes."

Quigs scoffed, "Women! You have no stamina."

Marina stumbled into the kitchen, one hand on her head and the other on her stomach. She glowered at Quigs.

"Wait till I feel better, Quigs. I'll show you stamina."

Esther slid an aspirin and a glass of water across the table.

"Fred used to have tomato juice with a raw egg and Worcestershire sauce in it when he'd overindulged, but due to the shortage of eggs, you'll have to make do with an aspirin for your head and a swig of baking soda for your stomach. If you have no objections and need no further nursing, then I'll get Joseph ready to go to Cora's. Be gentle with the girls, you two. I don't want a battle royal breaking out, and I don't want to see any blood spilt on my carpet when I get home."

)))

The nasty little man attacking my head with a sledgehammer and my stomach with a cement mixer eventually gave up his evil tasks, and allowed a brilliant idea to strike me. I paused while dusting the china cabinet.

"Marina, you know how Esther was saying about taking some carpet down to the shelter? I wonder if she has anything in her attic we could use to cheer the place up a bit. Because there's an awful lot of the blitz to go, not to mention the doodlebugs to come later on. Wouldn't that be a brilliant surprise for her?"

Marina's green (well, green and red today) eyes lit up. "That's wonderful! I wonder if Henry and Quigs have finished cleaning the shelter. Oh, I hope she has something up there we can use."

Quigs ran into the room.

"Henry and I had a brilliant idea. Why don't we go and see if there's anything in Esther's attic to brighten up the shelter?" he said.

"Hey, that's my idea!" I protested.

"Well, how nice to see that for once, you are in agreement," said Mr. Schmidt from the doorway. "Now, come along. We don't have a minute to spare if we are to do a good job. Assuming, of course, there is anything up there."

"Remember what happened the last time we went exploring," Marina reminded us. "We ended up sixty years in the past. Who knows where we'll end up if we go into the attic. Be funny if we ended up in Quigs' grandparents' house in the twenty-first century."

We hurried up the stairs. Mr. Schmidt opened the attic trapdoor and pulled down the ladder.

Like attics everywhere, this one was dark and dusty. I tried not to think about all the spiders probably lurking in the cracks and crevices.

Marina headed toward a sheet-shrouded pile in the corner.

"Bingo!" She shouted. "We've hit the jackpot here. Pictures, cushions, oh look! A couple of rugs."

Mr. Schmidt carefully unrolled the carpets. One was long and thin, obviously a section of stair runner, and the other was about five feet square. Both were slightly moth-eaten, but quite attractive in a heavy, old-fashioned way.

"Which one, children? The runner would fit between the bunks, maybe, and would probably extend to the door, but the square one would go under the bunks and not reach the door."

"Well, if the long one went right to the door, then it might get wet when it's raining, so I think the square one. I think the bunks might be a bit warmer in the winter if the cold didn't go through the floor, as well." I said.

If Mr. Schmidt was astounded at my unusual bout of brilliance, he was kind enough not to show it. "Well thought-out, Sophie. The square one it is. Roll them up, and put the runner back. Marina, what else do you have there?"

Marina looked up from cleaning her glasses on the hem of her blouse. "Some cushions and pictures. We could bang a nail in the framing across the back wall of the shelter and hang a picture on it."

Quigs sat silently flipping through photo albums, a look of wonder on his face. "I've found pictures of my family," he said softly. "Look, they must be my great-great-great-grandparents, or something."

We looked over his shoulder at the fading sepia prints of grim women in dresses with bustles and serious gentlemen in stiffly starched collars. He turned the pages, carefully smoothing the tissue paper between the photos. I had never seen Quigs so thoughtful before. He pointed to a picture of a tall young man in a military uniform, a sword hanging at his side. "Nathan Quigley 1875 – 1898," it said underneath the photo in ornate handwriting.

"He must have died in the Boer War in Africa," Mr. Schmidt said quietly. "Did you know that 'Nathan' was a family name, Quigs?"

Quigs shook his head, still staring at the photo. It must be spooky to see your name with a date of death beneath it.

"Why don't you bring those albums downstairs? I am sure Esther wouldn't mind if you look at them."

"What if it makes her ask all sorts of questions about my family?"

"Esther is a tactful person, and would not pry into matters you do not wish to discuss or which would make you feel uncomfortable. It is obvious to her from your appearance and your mannerisms that you are a Quigley, so that is enough for her. Take the albums downstairs and put them somewhere safe where Joseph can't get them."

Quigs climbed down the ladder, carefully clutching the albums to his chest.

"It's going to break his heart to go back," Marina said. "He seems so right here. He's totally different."

"Yes, it will be a shame for him to turn back into the angry young man we knew before. But assuming we manage to get back, he will have to adjust," Mr. Schmidt said. "And he will always have his memories. Now then, girls, you go down the ladder, I will bring the heavy items down."

As I stepped down to the landing, Quigs came out of his room. Tears had carved clean lines through the dust on his face. I looked down at my feet.

"You may want to wash your face, Quigs," I muttered.

"Look out below!" Mr. Schmidt tossed the cushions down. I hastily picked them up to allow him to come down with the carpet. "Just the picture to go now."

"See what else I found," he said after stowing the ladder away and closing the attic door. He held up an empty carved ivory picture frame.

"Someone get me a pencil and paper, and I shall see if I can make something nice for Esther."

Quigs, Marina, and I stood behind him as he drew. Within minutes, a likeness of Fred appeared under the pencil. To the left of Fred, Esther smiled out from the paper and Joseph laughed up at them from the lower right-hand corner.

"Oh, sir!" I breathed. "That's gorgeous! Esther will be pleased."

Mr. Schmidt studied his handiwork solemnly.

"I hope so, children. Because soon, things like this will be all she has of Fred. Oh, what am I thinking? This will be no substitute for her husband." His voice was sharp and bitter.

"No, it won't be a substitute for Fred. But every time she looks at it, she'll remember him, and she'll know how much we love her." I blinked furiously. "She'll know she's not alone."

"But she will be," Quigs replied angrily. "When we have to go home, she will be alone, except for Joseph. Now do you see why I must stay here? She'll need me. My parents will never need me."

Mr. Schmidt opened his mouth to speak and closed it again. Instead, he carefully placed the drawing behind the glass and replaced the back of the frame.

"Come, children. If we are to decorate the shelter before Esther returns, we must hurry. Time is marching on."

Of this fact, I was only too aware. Time was marching on. And for Fred, smiling from the frame in my hand, time was not marching on, but running out.

〉〉〉

"Did you have a nice time?" Esther asked, taking off her hat. "What did you eat?"

"Oh, Henry made us some vegetable thing. Really very nice. Oatmeal was a big part of it, but it was lovely and crunchy on top," I replied. "And how about you?"

Before she had a chance to reply, the siren started up.

Esther groaned. "Not again! Oh well, at least I made it home. It's not fun, running carrying one child on your hip and another in your tummy. Come on, let's go."

We stood aside to let Esther enter the shelter first.

"Oh my goodness, it's beautiful! The carpet from the attic, cushions, and—"

She picked up the sketch Mr. Schmidt had done, clapped her hand over her mouth and sat heavily on the bunk, never taking her eyes from the picture.

Quigs put his arm around Esther's shoulders.

"Esther? Don't you like it? Henry did it."

"It's beautiful," Esther whispered, touching it gently. "It's absolutely beautiful. I've never seen such a perfect, wonderful picture."

Mr. Schmidt cleared his throat. "It is only a little sketch, I'm afraid. I didn't have proper drawing pencils and good paper, but I wanted you to have a nice picture of your family."

Eyes swimming, Esther gazed up at Henry.

"Oh, thank you, Henry. As soon as Fred comes home, I'll show him. He'll thank you, too."

Fred had to come home. That was all there was to it. Somehow, we had to find Fred and bring him back to Esther, before it was too late.

CHAPTER 11

⟩⟩⟩ Monday, September 23, 1940

I was in that wonderful fuzzy half-world between awake and asleep. My pillow was soft and deep and the quilt billowed above me like a warm cloud. The war was a hundred light years away. Bliss. Absolute bliss.

Bliss exploded with a woman's shriek, blasting me bolt upright. Esther! What was wrong with Esther?

I grabbed my robe and headed to the bedroom door, Marina hot on my heels. Quigs was already clattering down the stairs.

Esther looked up the stairs at us, tears streaming down her face, a letter clutched in her hand. No! It couldn't be. It was too soon.

Then Esther started to laugh.

"Oh, it's wonderful! You won't believe it! Fred has been posted to Biggin Hill. He's just down the road. I'll be able to go and see him on the bus, and perhaps he can come here, if he's allowed off the base. But he's so close, so close!"

Quigs threw his arms around Esther.

"That's wonderful! Hey, maybe I can come with you and meet him. My uncle, the Spitfire hero. He's bound to be a hero, isn't he?"

Esther returned his hug and danced him around the hallway. "He's always been my hero, Quigs. I know he'll want to meet you."

Quigs charged up the stairs and banged on the bathroom door. "Henry! Fred's at Biggin Hill. Isn't it wonderful?"

Mr. Schmidt emerged, straightening his tie.

"Yes, Quigs, that is excellent news. Does he mention if he is able to get any leave at all, Esther?"

"No, he can't right now. Maybe in a few weeks, he says, if things settle down. Right now, it's enough for me to know he's so close." Esther changed track with her characteristic speed. "Oh! Breakfast time. And guess what? We've actually got some Weetabix. Oh, what a perfect day!"

She waltzed into the kitchen, singing. Her voice faded away behind the kitchen door. Mr. Schmidt followed.

"Well," Quigs said. "Now we know where he is. We've got to make a plan to get him back here."

"We can't," Marina said, dejected. "You know we can't change history. It's not allowed."

"Not allowed by whom? Who made the rules about time travel? Anyway, it might be a better future if Fred lives. It'll certainly be better for Esther, Fred, and Joseph. Anyway, I'm going to try to save his life. You two can let him die if you like, but I'm going to do everything I can to save him." He thought a minute. "I'm going out to see him . . . today."

Marina and I stared at him.

"So are you with me or not?"

"I'm in."

"Me too."

"Right. This is what we'll do—"

〉〉〉

"Is anyone looking out a window?" I whispered hoarsely.

Marina peeked out of the shed.

"I don't see anyone, but who's to say who's lurking behind those curtains? I think Mrs. Jones has eyes in the back of her head."

I giggled. "I think her radar's tuned to Mr. Schmidt's frequency, though. She only calls out when he's going by, never when we are. And he's safely in his classroom by now. We'd better go quickly, before Esther finishes bathing Joseph."

We swiftly wheeled the bikes from the shed, through the garden, and out into the back alley. With high garden walls on one side of us and the railway embankment on the other, we were quite well hidden.

"Look! There's Quigs," I said to Marina. "Oh, my goodness, he's brought Bert with him. I thought he was only going to borrow Bert's bike."

"Get a move on! I feel like an idiot standing here with a girl's bike. It belongs to Bert's sister. Thought you'd prefer a bike without a cross-bar," Quigs offered.

"Thanks. Is Bert coming with us?" I asked.

"Yes. He says he knows some shortcuts to Biggin Hill," Quigs explained.

"Hurry up," Bert said crossly. "We can't stand around the alley all day. You girls are supposed to be in school, even if we're not. How long do you think it'll take for one of these nosy neighbors to report to Esther that you're skulking around the alley? We'd better get moving. Biggin Hill's about ten miles, and it's hilly. Reckon you ladies can make it?"

"I'll give you 'ladies'," I grunted, jumping on my bike. Pedaling hard, I sped past him.

"Who's the little lady now?" I called over my shoulder.

It was a perfect day for biking—cool, crisp, and sunny. We rode through familiar streets in companionable silence for most of the way. Except for the occasional gutted house or crater in the road, we could easily forget we were in 1940 and on what was literally a life-or-death mission. I pulled alongside Quigs.

"Have you thought about what you're going to say to Fred? Are you just going to say 'Hello, I'm your long-lost third cousin five times removed, and I'm living in your house?' "

Quigs looked at me miserably. "Don't laugh, Soph. I honestly don't have a clue what I'm going to say. How about 'Oh hello, Fred. Don't go up on Friday night or you'll die. Oh, and incidentally, I know this for a fact because I'm really your great-grandson.' "

"Why not simply tell him to come round on Friday night? Maybe he could get some special leave, or something."

"Get leave in the middle of the blitz?" Quigs shook his head. "Not likely. All I know is, we have one chance to save him. We have to get it right."

〉〉〉

"Well, this is it," Bert announced unnecessarily. "Biggin on the Bump."

We dismounted and stared at the forbidding headquarters building. Now what?

With a quiet determination and dignity I'd never seen in him before, Quigs left his bike on the roadside and strode over to the guard at the gate.

"Good morning," I heard him say. "My name is Nathan Quigley, and I would like to see a relative of mine, Flying Officer Frederick Quigley." He paused. "Please."

"Oh, you would, would you? And I'm supposed to tell him to leave his duties and drop everything to see you, am I?"

"I'll only keep him a minute. I have . . . I have an important message from his wife, Mrs. Esther Quigley."

"I'm sorry, son. But I can't fetch him for you. My C.O. would have my guts for garters. And I don't even know if he's here." The guard didn't sound unkind, only extremely tired. "Best you go home and get Mrs. Quigley to write him a nice letter."

The guard turned to a WAAF crossing the compound with a clipboard and binoculars as three Spitfires approached the aerodrome, the engine on the rear plane sputtering loudly.

"Who's that coming in now?" he called.

She raised her binoculars. "Henderson, Bailey and Quigley. At last. Oh, I don't like the sound of Quigley's engine. Coming in on a wing and a prayer, as usual. Anyway, that's the last of them counted in."

Quigs turned and raced back to his bike.

"Come on!" he shouted. "Maybe if they stop close to a fence, we can see Fred."

Black smoke billowed from Fred's engine. Its bell ringing urgently, a fire engine raced to the landing strip.

"Hey, you!" the guard shouted to us. "Ride down about two hundred yards. You may be close enough to see him."

We hurtled down the road as fast as we could go. The first two planes had landed and had taxied off the runway. I don't know how Fred could even see the runway through the dense black cloud swirling from the front of his plane. A tongue of fire licked the cockpit window.

"He's down!" Quigs yelled, leaping off his bike before he'd even come to a stop.

The Spitfire slowly drew to halt. Fred climbed from the cockpit and jumped down from the wing. Laughing, he pulled off his goggles.

"At least you keep us in business, Quigley," one of the firemen called as he turned his hose on the plane.

"I like to do my bit for the war economy," Fred shouted back. "I keep all the girls in the aircraft factories busy."

"Fred!" Quigs screamed, at the top of his lungs. "Fred! Over here! I have a message from Esther."

Fred stopped in his tracks and ran towards us.

"You must be the kids Esther wrote to me about. Is she okay? Nothing's happened to her, has it?"

My heart skipped a beat as I gazed up at him. No wonder Esther was so in love. And Quigs might look like this when he grows up. Interesting.

"No, no, she's fine. She got your letter this morning and she's so excited you're at Biggin Hill now. She'd really love you to come for dinner on Friday night. Oh, please say you'll come. She has something extremely important to tell you." Quigs shifted anxiously from foot to foot.

Fred sighed and shook his head. "Leave is out of the question at the moment. I'm overdue for a forty-eight hour leave, but it keeps being cancelled. You're sure she's okay? And Joseph?"

Marina broke in. "They're both fine. I'm afraid we neglected to tell Esther we were coming to see you today so she couldn't send a message, but I am sure both Esther and Joseph would have sent lots of love had they known we were coming."

Fred laughed. "Playing hooky, eh? Is Bert here teaching you his tricks? Surprised you got away with it. I thought Esther said your guardian was a teacher. I suppose he doesn't know yet, either. Wouldn't want to be in your shoes tonight."

One of the other pilots strode over. "Who's this then, Quigley? Is this your son?"

"Not that I know of, sir. These are the kids I told you about, the ones my wife took in." He paused. "I'm sorry; I can't remember your names. I know you're Quigs."

"I'm Marina Curtis, and this is my friend Sophie Pinkerton. Quigs' real name is Nathan." Marina took a breath and turned her emerald eyes on the other man. "We were hoping to be able to persuade Flying Officer Quigley to come to dinner at Esther's on Friday. It's rather urgent that she sees him."

The man smiled. "I'm sure it is. But you might have noticed there's a war on and under the present circumstances, all leave has been cancelled. But assuming Jerry behaves himself, Esther is more than welcome to come here on Saturday afternoon. We're showing a film and the men can each bring a civilian guest."

Saturday would be too late.

Marina gazed up at the man, her eyes glistening with tears behind her glasses. "Are you sure, sir? Can't he ask his boss?"

Fred laughed. "This is my boss, Marina. This is Wing Commander Henderson."

Oops.

"How long has it been since you've had leave, Quigley?" Henderson asked.

"My last forty-eight was three months ago, sir."

"Tell you what. For some reason, it seems to be of the utmost importance that Esther sees you on Friday night. What if you go and see her for a few hours? That's the best I can do, I'm afraid. Actually, there's a young lady in Penge I wouldn't mind seeing. We can drive in together."

"Oh, that's wonderful!" I cried, jumping up and down. "Thank you so much. Esther will be thrilled."

"Best you don't tell her," Fred said. "Just in case something goes wrong. I don't want her to be disappointed. And that way, I can surprise her. One more thing. This teacher—he's not good-looking, is he?"

Once again, Marina saved the day. "Not compared to you, sir. Anyway, Esther's always talking about you. She's told us you're the only man in the world for her, and you always will be. And as for Henry, his real ambition is to be a Catholic priest, so you have no worries there."

I nearly choked.

"That's all right then. Well, I'll see you Friday about seven o'clock." He grinned at Quigs. "I don't know what relation you are, but you're obviously a Quigley. Look after Esther for me."

Quigs nodded solemnly. "I will. I promise." He stood at attention and snapped a salute.

"Good man." Fred returned the salute, turned and walked away with the Wing Commander.

Bert gazed after them, shaking his head.

"You shouldn't do it, you know."

"Do what?" I demanded.

"Try to change things. You just shouldn't do it."

Bert knew. He simply had to.

"What do you mean, Bert? Try to change what?"

This was his cue to say we shouldn't try to change the future, that we can't, that Fred will die, that we'll never get back. Instead, he looked at me mockingly and said, "Air force regulations, of course. You shouldn't try to change them. They're written in stone. Like the past and the future; you shouldn't try to change them."

He climbed on his bike and started for home.

CHAPTER 12

⟩⟩⟩ Friday, September 27, 1940

The next few days passed in a blur. Quigs lived in a state of high excitement. Ever since seeing him land the burning plane, Fred had become his hero. Not being able to tell Mr. Schmidt and Esther—or anyone else, come to think of it—about our adventure must have been driving him crazy. Whenever we were alone, it was "Fred this" and "Fred that," until you would have thought Fred had defeated the Luftwaffe single-handed and had still made it home in time for lunch.

I dried the last plate and stacked it in the cupboard.

"Do you think we're doing the right thing, Marina? Changing history, I mean. Because we are, aren't we? If Fred doesn't die tonight, then we've changed history. Who knows what will happen?"

"He's only one man. What difference can one ordinary man make to the future of the world? That's what I keep telling myself, anyway. Well, we've done it now. We can't very well go and uninvite him, can we? He'll be here in half an hour."

"Who'll be here in half an hour?" Esther asked, coming inside with a basket of washing.

"Bert," I replied quickly. "I asked him over to help me with my math homework but I don't feel like doing it now."

"I don't blame you. Math on a Friday night. Not my idea of fun."

"But since he's coming, why don't we have a dance like we did on Saturday? Oh, come on Esther. Do say yes! You could teach us some more steps. And you could wear that lovely dress again."

"Well, it would be fun to dress up. We don't get many opportunities with this blasted war, and I suppose the ironing will still be here tomorrow."

Quigs charged into the kitchen as Esther's footsteps faded up the stairs. He pulled a paper bag out of his school bag.

"You won't believe what Bert's mother made for Fred and Esther for tonight. Bert says you don't want to know where she got the ingredients."

I peeped in the bag. I couldn't believe my eyes—chocolate éclairs, bursting with whipped cream and slathered with smooth chocolate icing. Hopefully, Fred and Esther wouldn't have any qualms about eating black-market goods. My mouth watering, I carefully set the pastries on two of Esther's best bone china plates.

The front door slammed.

We really should have told Mr. Schmidt what we had done. I darted through the connecting door to the dining room where Mr. Schmidt was marking homework.

"That's Fred at the door," I whispered quickly. "We've told him you want to be a Catholic priest."

Mr. Schmidt looked at me as if I'd taken leave of my senses, but I was used to that.

"I'll explain everything later. The important thing is, we met Fred and he was worried about you being good-looking. Marina said you wanted to be a priest so he wouldn't be jealous. Come on!"

I dragged him to his feet.

Fred and Wing Commander Henderson filled the front hall with their blue serge shoulders. Joseph hurtled down the stairs and flung himself at Fred, who swung him high in the air.

Esther, a look of wonder on her face, appeared at the top of the stairs. For a split second, you could have heard a pin drop. Fred gently set Joseph down on the floor, plopped his cap on Joseph's copper curls and bounded up the stairs two at a time, Joseph hot on his heels.

"Well, I'm certainly surplus to requirements," Henderson commented. "I'm off to see a friend in Penge. I'll be back at nine."

Nine. I shot a worried look at Quigs. That might not be late enough.

Esther and Fred came slowly down the stairs, their arms around each other's waists. Joseph raced up and down the hallway, arms out airplane style, squealing loudly.

Fred cut off Esther's attempt at introductions with a kiss. "I've met the children already. Who do you think told me you had some important news?" He turned to Mr. Schmidt and held out his hand, distrust in his eyes. "I assume you're the teacher fellow."

"Yes, I am Henry Smith, the teacher fellow as you say. At least I am for now. As soon as this war ends, I intend to enter the church, possibly even become a Trappist monk."

Esther's face was a picture.

"Well, that's all right then." Fred shook Mr. Schmidt's hand and slapped him on the back. "I don't want to seem rude, but I only have two hours—"

"I quite understand. Children, in the kitchen, please."

Marina hummed "The Funeral March" under her breath. We were doomed.

Mr. Schmidt quietly shut the kitchen door and turned to face us. "Would someone care to explain?"

"Well, sir, we sort of—bumped into Fred, you see."

"Bumped into Fred? Sophie, where did you manage to bump into Fred?"

"Biggin Hill," I whispered.

"Where?"

"Biggin Hill, sir." Louder that time. Oh, what was the use? I might as well tell him the whole story—how Marina and I skipped school, how we borrowed the bikes, how we rode all the way to Biggin Hill, how we decided to try to change history.

"So you see, Henry, we've saved Fred's life and now Joseph and his little brother or sister will have a father, and Esther will be happy forever, and everything will be as it should be." I couldn't stop the tears rolling down my cheeks.

"Oh, Sophie, Sophie. Everything will not be as it should be. Fred should die. I know that sounds horrible, but that is what happened and what should happen. Fred . . . should . . . die."

At that moment, I hated Mr. Schmidt.

"We've gone over this time and time again. Who knows what domino effect this will have? Fred is only one man, insignificant outside his immediate family and circle of friends, but his life—or his death—might have made a difference. Suppose tonight he would have shot down a bomber on its way to destroy central London or an important military target or even just another part of the East End. Suppose now because Fred isn't up there, that bomber gets through. Because you chose to interfere in history, the entire course of the war could be changed and hundreds of people could be killed or injured."

Quigs' voice was icy and resolute. "I don't care. I don't care if Churchill gets bombed tonight, or the King, or anyone else. All I care about is my family. My family, do you hear? I've never had a family to care about before and now that I do, you're telling me I should let one of them die. I'm glad we did what we did. I know it was the right thing to do."

"Did you see their faces?" Marina said softly, her green eyes even brighter than ever with unshed tears. "If ever two people belonged together, it's Esther and Fred. I'm sorry, sir, if you think we've let you down or if you think we've done wrong, but I agree with Sophie and Quigs. We did the right thing and I'd do it all again, in a heartbeat." She gave a very un-Marina-like sniff and blew her nose hard.

Joseph bounded in.

"Mummy says can she have a cup of tea please, and I'm to stay in here until it's ready. Mummy says to make it really strong for Daddy."

"I think that translates to 'Mummy wants some time alone with Daddy'," I laughed, filling the kettle and putting it on much lower heat than normal.

The heavy, ominous ticking of the kitchen clock filled the room, counting the seconds until Fred had to go. Was it ticking away the seconds until Fred had to die? *No.* Don't think that way. This had to work. It simply had to.

Marina's voice broke into my thoughts. "Sophie, you can stand a spoon up in that tea. I think it's ready."

I set the tea tray as prettily as possible with a lace tray cloth and Esther's best china. Joseph's eyes widened at the sight of the éclairs.

"Mummy! Daddy!" he shouted, tearing into the sitting room. "Look what we have!"

I put the tray down on the table. "The éclairs are from Mrs. Martin. Bert said not to ask about the ingredients."

Fred laughed. "Do you have any objections to black-market food, darling?"

Esther gazed at him adoringly. "I don't have any objections to anything tonight."

The air-raid siren screamed.

"Except that. Oh blast that rotten siren!"

Someone was pounding on the front door.

Wing Commander Henderson's voice drifted in from the front hall. "Sorry to interrupt, but we have to fly. Literally. Come on, Quigley."

This couldn't be happening.

Fred rose to his feet and took his cap off Joseph's head.

"No, Daddy, don't go!"

"I have to, Joseph." His face bleak, he kissed Joseph and held Esther tightly.

"I'll see you tomorrow at the movies, darling?" he asked Esther.

She nodded, tears welling in her eyes.

"Daddy, don't go!" Joseph's screams nearly drowned out the wailing siren.

"I'm sorry, son, I have to. Mummy can bring you to Biggin Hill one day, and I'll show you my plane."

"Come on, Quigley. If we step on it, we should be back at the base in twenty minutes."

No. Don't go. *Don't go.*

The clock struck eight.

Fred kissed Esther one more time and he was gone.

CHAPTER 13

⟫⟫⟫ Saturday, September 28, 1940

The raid lasted until six in the morning—nine and a half hours. Hours filled with wondering, dreading, hoping. Hours spent feeling sure that since Fred had taken off at a different time than he should have, he would be okay. He would live. Hours spent despairing, knowing we'd failed and he would die.

Esther had been happy and excited all night long, speaking of seeing Fred again on Saturday afternoon, of holding hands and snuggling in the back row of the theater.

Joseph had been bouncier than ever, and had hardly slept. Every ten minutes, he asked if it was time to see Daddy's plane yet.

Mr. Schmidt sat silently, his face desolate.

"Oh, come on, Henry, what are you looking so serious about?" Esther dug him in the ribs. "So what if the children took off from school for one day. Please don't be angry with them. I think what they did was wonderful. They gave me the best present I could ever have. Well, short of having Fred home for good, that is. I wish the all clear would hurry up and blow. If I don't get some sleep, I'm going to look like a real fright this afternoon, and Fred will wonder what on earth he's married."

Another rumbling wave of engines surged closer. Would they ever stop? At least they were all going over without dropping their loads on us.

Esther and Joseph finally fell into an uneasy sleep, curled up together on one narrow bunk. Her gold hair and his bright copper curls glowed like flames in the dancing candlelight.

"Do you think it worked?" Quigs whispered.

I shook my head slowly. "I don't know, Quigs. I hope so. I expect we'll find out soon enough."

)))

The clock in the sitting room struck eleven.

No news was good news. Or so I hoped, anyway.

With my stomach tied in nervous knots, I asked Mr. Schmidt how and when they notified women that their husbands had died.

"By telegram, usually. I believe a boy on a bicycle normally brings it. I don't know how quickly they get the news to them, though. I suppose it depends on whether they know the man is actually dead or whether they think he's missing in action. But I imagine it would take a day or so."

"Would you stop it?" Quigs said angrily, his face pale and tense. "He's not dead, so there's no point to this conversation. Esther will go to Biggin Hill this afternoon and they'll have a wonderful time. You'll see."

We froze as a knock on the front door echoed around the hallway.

Joseph charged down the stairs shouting, "Daddy! Daddy! Daddy's car's outside. I saw it from my window."

Quigs raced to the door and tore it open.

Wing Commander Henderson stood there, grim-faced—alone.

"Where's Daddy? Is he hiding?" Joseph demanded.

"May I come in? I need to speak to Mrs. Quigley."

"Quigs, go and get Esther's sister Cora as quickly as you can," Mr. Schmidt said. "Marina, make some tea, hot and sweet. Move!"

Esther appeared on the upstairs landing, just as she had yesterday evening. She ran lightly down the stairs.

"Hello! What brings you here? If Fred asked you to pick me up, I'm afraid I'm nowhere near ready. The raid last night went on and on."

"Mrs. Quigley—Esther—I'm afraid I have some bad news. May we go into the sitting room?"

"But where's Daddy?" Joseph demanded again.

Mr. Schmidt picked Joseph up and held him tightly. "Come into the kitchen, little one. Let's see if Marina can find you a biscuit."

"Sophie?" Esther blinked with bewilderment and held out her hand. I led her gently to the sofa and sat beside her, wishing I was anywhere but here.

Henderson studied Fred's photo on the mantel for a moment. He sighed deeply and turned to face us.

"Esther, I'm afraid something terrible has happened. I felt I owed it to Fred and to you to tell you in person."

"No. No." Esther's lips were tight and bloodless.

"Esther, there's no easy way to say this. Last night, Fred's aircraft took heavy fire and was shot down."

"Shot down where? Over England? In Kent or Sussex? If I know Fred, he's probably charming some farmer's wife and eating breakfast."

"No, Esther, I'm afraid he was shot down over the English Channel. As you said, the raids last night were very heavy and lasted a long time. Over fifty German raids headed to London from Cherbourg and Dieppe in France. During the course of intercepting those raids, he was shot down."

"But maybe a boat has picked him up," Esther said. "Surely there're lots of boats in the Channel. They'll find him soon. I know they will." Her nails dug into my hand so hard that a crescent of blood appeared on my palm.

"Esther, I'm so sorry. I was above him when—when it happened. I saw it. I'm afraid he did not survive. I am so very, very sorry. If it helps, before he was shot down, he definitely hit two German planes, possibly three."

"He shot down two German planes, possibly three," Esther repeated softly, looking down. Her head jerked up, her mouth twisted into a grimace. Her voice remained cool and controlled, deathly quiet. "And that's supposed to make me feel better, Wing Commander Henderson? I'm supposed to feel better knowing that definitely two women in Germany, possibly three, are feeling what I'm feeling right now? I'm supposed to feel better knowing that they hate my husband as much as I hate theirs? And that's supposed to make me feel better, Wing Commander Henderson, *sir?* Because it doesn't."

Marina appeared in the doorway, carrying a tea tray set just as it had been the evening before, with the lace cloth and best bone china. Only the éclairs were missing.

Esther took the cup mechanically, gripping it so hard that it shattered in her hand. She gazed mutely at the tea stains on her dress and peered at the red scald mark on her hand, holding her fingers apart, staring at her hand as if she'd never seen it before.

The front door burst open. Esther rose to her feet looking tired and old as Cora and Quigs ran into the room. Cora gathered Esther into her arms, stroking her hair and rocking her backwards and forwards, like she was a child.

Wing Commander Henderson wiped his hand across his face. "If there's anything I can do—anything at all."

Cora looked up. "Thank you. You've been very kind, I'm sure."

Henderson had obviously been dismissed.

"Are you sure?" Quigs asked Henderson, pulling on his sleeve as they stood at the front door. "Are you absolutely sure?"

Henderson nodded. "Yes, son, I'm sure." He looked across at Mr. Schmidt. "Where's Joseph?"

"He fell asleep on my lap. He didn't get much sleep last night. I've put him down on some blankets in the kitchen. There is absolutely no hope, I assume."

"No. I couldn't tell Esther what I saw. It would have been too much for her. Several bullets penetrated the canopy of the aircraft. He would have been killed instantly, which was a blessing as the plane went up in a fireball. I am sorry to say there's no way he could have survived."

I clapped my hand over my mouth and ran, retching and heaving, into the kitchen. Gasping, I hung onto the sink and rinsed the vomit down the drain.

Marina handed me a glass of water and a hankie.

"Come on. Rinse. Blow."

We clung together for a moment, our tears mingling.

Marina took off her glasses and wiped her eyes with the back of her hand. "We have to be strong, Sophie. I know that sounds like something out of a bad book or an old film. But we do. We have to be strong for Esther and Joseph—and Quigs. We're this upset and we barely knew Fred. Imagine what they're feeling."

I looked out of the window at Quigs throwing stones at the railway embankment. He turned to find another missile, his face contorted with anguish and fury.

"What should we do, Marina?" I whispered.

She shook her head sadly.

The back gate opened and Bert strode through. Quigs turned back to the embankment, hastily wiped his face with the back of his hand, and then faced Bert. Quigs said something; I couldn't hear what. The two boys looked at each other for a moment and went back to hurling stones.

I looked down at Joseph, curled up like a kitten on the pile of blankets. The sun streaming through the window shone on his halo of curls.

"How's Esther going to tell him?"

"The same way mothers across England, Germany, France, and Holland—mothers all over Europe tell their children their daddy isn't coming home." She shook her head again, her voice cracking. "I don't know, Sophie. I just don't know."

❭ ❭ ❭

I've never had such a horrible day in my life.

Nobody looked anyone else in the eye, not wanting to see their own pain reflected there. Cora asked Esther and Joseph to stay with her, but Esther refused, saying she wasn't leaving Fred's house. Together, Cora and Esther told Joseph his daddy was dead. Joseph simply stared at them, and asked when it would be time to go and see his daddy's plane.

❭ ❭ ❭

We sat silently in the Anderson shelter that night. Joseph had finally grasped what had happened and had cried himself to sleep, his head on Quigs' lap. Quigs, his face as hard as marble, ran his fingers over Joseph's hair. Esther paced like a caged lion, up and down, up and down. Three steps. Turn. Three steps. Turn.

The rumble of planes grew louder, peppered with bursts of anti-aircraft gunfire. Bombs were falling ever nearer. I was grateful Joseph could sleep through this cacophony. I sat with my elbows on my knees, my hands over my ears.

Three steps. Turn. Three steps. Esther tore open the shelter door and darted outside. Screaming loudly, Joseph sat bolt upright. Quigs and Marina clutched him tightly as he tried to make a dash for his mother.

Esther stood in the middle of the carrot patch, shaking her fists at the heavens.

"Stop it!" she screamed. "Stop it! Do you hear me? Just—please—stop it!"

She wrapped her arms around herself and fell to her knees in the mud, sobs wracking her body.

Mr. Schmidt charged out and drew Esther gently to her feet and held her, cradling her head against his shoulder. Behind them, a bomb screamed earthward. The earth shook. Against the fiery glow, I saw the ghostly shadow of another bomb hurtling down. And another. Mr. Schmidt and Esther stood like statues, silhouetted against the blazing sky. Hot shrapnel hailed down and bounced off the path. His right arm around her shoulder and his left hand shielding her bowed head, Mr. Schmidt steered Esther firmly to the safety of the shelter. I shut the door behind them. Freed from Quigs' and Marina's restraint, Joseph launched himself at Esther, burying his face in her dress. She gently stroked his hair with one hand, her other hand resting on her stomach. She looked up, a faint glimmer of hope flickering like the glow of a guttering candle through her tears.

"The baby," she said. "It moved. That was the first time I felt the baby move."

Mr. Schmidt, Quigs, and Marina gathered around Esther and showered her with congratulations.

I stood silently by myself. This was all wrong. Esther should be curled up with Joseph and Fred at this moment, not cooped up in a tin can, her husband lying—*no.* Don't finish that sentence.

I wept.

CHAPTER 14

⟩⟩⟩ Sunday, October 13, 1940

In the days and weeks following Fred's death, we fell into a dull routine of school, air raids, and chores. The sun no longer shone from Esther. Her face became tight and drawn and her eyes lost their sparkle. She walked around the house like a robot—cooking, cleaning, smiling at Quigs' rotten jokes, laughing at Joseph's antics—but she was no longer the shining young woman she'd been a short time ago. She was becoming one of those drab, hollow-eyed women who constantly queued for rations outside the High Street shops.

Marina sighed deeply as we stared at the rain lashing against the sitting room window. "We can't let it go on, Soph. She's running herself into the ground."

"But what else can we do? We've taken over the gardening for her, Quigs puts Joseph to bed and reads him a story at night, and Henry makes sure she doesn't do any really heavy cleaning."

"It's not the physical work that's the problem. She lived for Fred, and now he's gone. Before, she thrived on being busy. Being pregnant and all, it can't be easy waking up and going to the shelter every night. Hey, that's an Air Force staff car pulling up. Wonder what's going on?"

Part of me dreamed Fred had ejected from his aircraft, had been fished out of the channel, and had come home. Most of me knew otherwise.

I sprinted to the front door and yanked it open before we heard a knock.

A motherly WAAF officer stood on the doorstep, her hand poised to grab the knocker. "My goodness, that's quick service. You'd make an excellent butler. Is Mrs. Esther Quigley at home? Sergeant Elizabeth Mayweather to see her." She stepped inside, not giving me a chance to answer.

Esther came out of the kitchen, drying her hands on her apron. On seeing Sergeant Mayweather, she blanched and clutched the newel post for support.

"Is it Fred? Is he back?"

Sergeant Mayweather bustled forward, took Esther firmly by the arm and steered her into the sitting room.

"No, sorry, my dear. I wish I could bring news like that, but I can't. I'm Betty Mayweather. Most of the pilots on the squadron call me 'auntie.' I'm the one they come to when their love lives need sorting out, or they've had bad news from home, all that sort of thing. And I'm the one your husband gave this letter to at the beginning of the war."

Esther stared at the older woman, open-mouthed.

"The afternoon of September 27th, the day Fred was shot down, I was ill. Ruptured appendix. They rushed me off to hospital and then shipped me home to recuperate. I've been stuck in the wilds of Northumbria, totally cut off from civilization. Got back to base yesterday, and found out what had happened to young Fred. Oh my dear, I am so terribly, terribly sorry for your loss. Fred was wonderful—pleasant, polite, funny, clever. He adored you. Talked about you constantly. It was Esther this, Esther that. Totally devoted. When he found we were to be posted to Biggin Hill, he was beside himself with joy at the thought of being closer to you. Thrilled to pieces! Anyway, he wrote this letter ages ago, just in case anything happened. I always hoped I'd be able to tear it up at the end of the war. Here. Take it. It won't bite."

Esther slowly took the envelope and held it close to her chest. "I'll read it later, if you don't mind," she whispered.

"Of course, my dear. Well, I'll be off now. Leave you to read your letter in peace. Don't bother getting up. I can find the door."

I shut the front door behind the sergeant and peeped in at Esther. She sat like a statue, holding the envelope in both hands, staring at it.

She looked up.

"I don't want to open it, Soph. I can only open this envelope once. I can read the letter over and over, but I can only actually open the envelope once."

"Then wait," Marina said softly from behind me. "Wait until the time is absolutely right to open it. Simply having that letter in your hands tells you how much he loved you."

Esther rose slowly to her feet, and walked to the mirror above the mantel. She ran her hand over her lank hair and smoothed a line on her face.

"Old," she said, her voice dull and expressionless. "I look old. Fred wouldn't want me to look this way, to be this way. Fred called me his ray of sunshine."

"Would you like me to help you to wash and set your hair?" Marina offered. "We could have a beauty session."

Esther turned from the mirror and smiled faintly. It was weak and wobbly, but it was the closest thing to a genuine smile I had seen on her face since Fred's death. She tucked the letter carefully inside the pocket of her apron. She swallowed hard and brushed her eyes with the back of her hand. She spoke with quiet resignation.

"I saw a new hairstyle in *Woman's Own* that I'd like to try. Come on, girls. Make me beautiful again."

CHAPTER 15

))) Monday, October 14, 1940

I noticed the girl standing by herself by the school gates because she looked like I did in a strange, new situation—scared, uncomfortable and very alone. Most of the girls stared at her curiously and walked by. I could feel her stomach churning and could taste the fear in her mouth.

"Hello! I'm Sophie Pinkerton. What's your name?"

Relief shone in her eyes. She held out her hand.

"My name is Ruth Weismann."

My jaw dropped at her accent. She was German.

Seeing the change in my expression, the joy drained from her face and the shutters closed in her eyes.

"Yes, I am German. You had better go, hadn't you? You can't be seen talking to a German girl, can you?"

"I can talk to anyone I like. Come with me; I'll introduce you to my friends, Pru and Marina. So, have you recently come from Germany? If I'm not being nosy. My mother says—said—that I always ask too many questions."

"I came just before the war. My parents sent me to live with my auntie in Bethnal Green. They couldn't get out themselves, but they made sure I was safe."

"Oh! Where are your parents now?" I asked, unthinking.

Ruth swallowed and shrugged, shaking her head. "I don't know," she whispered. "A camp in the East somewhere."

No. Oh no.

I linked my arm through hers and blinking away hot tears, led her over to Pru and Marina.

"Hey, Jew Girl," came Gert's taunting voice. "I'd stay away from those two if I were you. They're Nazis."

Ruth pulled away. Pru put her hand on Ruth's arm.

"Don't mind ghastly Gert. She's had it in for Sophie and Marina ever since they started here. And sadly, it looks like you've joined her list of enemies. I don't know what's to be done with that girl."

"Wherever I go, it's the same. Some people don't like me because I'm German. Some people don't like me because I'm a Jew. And then some people *really* don't like me because I'm a German Jew. I suppose that is how it will be forever."

"No it won't," Marina said confidently.

Pru and Ruth stared at her.

"Well, it won't, will it? This war has to end sometime. Anyway, if you moved to Bethnal Green, what are you doing in Beckenham?"

"My aunt was bombed out, so I was sent to live with yet another aunt and uncle here. The house is by the tram depot. Do you know where that is?"

I replied, "Yes, that's not too far from where Pru lives. Come on, we'll walk you home. We have to make a slight detour though, past the boys' school. Our friend is plowing the school vegetable garden, and we have to heckle him."

All the way down the street, I could feel Gert behind us. She kept a steady five paces back; if we slowed down, she slowed down. If we sped up, she sped up.

"That girl's really getting to me," I muttered. "I'm going to thump her one day, I really will."

"This is the boys' school," Pru told Ruth. "Oh look—there's Quigs! My goodness, that plow's quite the contraption, isn't it?"

Six boys pulled the handmade plow, and two guided it from the back. They were doing quite well; the furrows were straight and they were going at a breakneck pace. Until they saw Marina, that is.

"Hey, Quigs!" Marina shouted, jumping up and down.

The two boys guiding the plow jerked their heads around and lost their grip on the handles. The blade dug deep into the ground.

The plow lurched sideways and ground to an abrupt halt, depositing all eight boys face down in the mud.

"Oops," said Marina weakly.

"Oh, to have that effect on men, eh, Ruth?" Pru dug Ruth in the ribs, chortling loudly. "And she's only twelve."

Gert was still five paces away.

Mr. Schmidt, who had been supervising, called over, "That will teach you boys to watch where you're going. Has anyone hurt anything other than his pride?"

Gert stood between Ruth and me, and put her arms chummily about our shoulders. She hissed in Ruth's ear in a German accent, "There's your real enemy, Jew Girl. See him? Is he not the Master Race, *ja?* Is he not a Nazi, *ja?*"

That was it. I snapped. I threw down my school bag and my gas mask, and jerked my elbow back to Gert's stomach. I spun around, and landed a right hook to her jaw.

"Whoa! Fight!" I heard one of the boys shout, as Gert tugged my hair fiercely. I kicked her hard in the shins.

"Stop it at once!" Stepping between us, Mr. Schmidt pushed us apart. "Stop it! Who would care to tell me the meaning of this disgraceful behavior?"

I was too filled with rage to speak. Gert was still glaring at me, teeth bared like a wildcat, breathing hard.

"It was my fault, sir," Ruth said quietly. "I am afraid Sophie was coming to my defense. Had I not been here, this would not have happened."

"Oh yes it would," I said through gritted teeth. "Sooner or later, this would have happened. Gert's been pushing me ever since I met her."

Mr. Schmidt ignored me and looked at Ruth. "And why was Sophie defending you? What did Gert say?" His accent, as it always was when he was angry, was very strong—very German.

"Nothing. It was nothing. Truly," Ruth demurred.

I had never seen such terror in a person's face before, and I hoped I never would again.

The boys had come closer. I could feel their eyes boring into us. Without turning around, Mr. Schmidt said, "Go on, you lot. Clean yourselves up and make sure you leave the lavatories spotless."

"Girls, let's carry on this discussion in the headmaster's study. He has left for the day, for which you should be thankful, but I am sure he would rather we discuss this in the school and not on the pavement. Yes, Pru and Marina, you too. Hopefully, you can shed some light on what happened."

From the fence to the school was the longest fifty yards I have ever walked. Oh, how I wished Gert had never been born.

Mr. Schmidt shut the study door and leaned against the desk. "So," he said softly, "who will start?"

"I don't have to talk to you," Gert sneered. "Rotten German."

"Ah, but you do have to talk to me, Gertrude Pratt. You were in a fight at my school, so to me, you will explain. And for the record, I am not German, but Swiss."

"Sound German to me," Gert muttered.

Pru dove in. "Gert has tormented Sophie and Marina ever since they started at the school. For some reason, she took it into her head they're German spies at worst, sympathizers at best. Personally, I feel they've shown great restraint in not clobbering her before. Blimey, I've come near to it once or twice. Today, Ruth here joined the school. Ruth is Jewish and was evacuated from Germany just before the war. Gert has extended her hate campaign to Ruth. Actually, sir, you might have noticed it extends to you as well. To be honest, I can't think of anyone she *does* like. Anyway, she called Ruth 'Jew Girl' and said you were a Nazi. So Sophie belted her. That's it. End of story, sir."

"Is that right, Sophie?"

I nodded.

He looked at Ruth. Very gently he asked, "And your parents, Ruth? I assume they didn't get out?"

She shook her head, whispering, "No, sir."

"Are they in a camp?"

"Yes, sir."

He closed his eyes and sighed deeply, his face bleak.

"Pru, would you be kind enough to walk Ruth home? She doesn't need to be here."

The door closed behind them.

"Right, Gert. What do you know about concentration camps?"

She shrugged.

"Well, shall I tell you, then? Shall I tell you of the suffering, the humiliation, the starvation? Shall I tell you of the deaths? And why? Because of peoples' race and what they believe in. All because other people are narrow-minded, bigoted, and see only what they want to see. Because people are afraid of what they do not understand and because people think they are better than others. Gertrude, do you think you are better than Ruth? Do you think you are more deserving of care and respect?"

She stood silently, tracing a pattern on the carpet with her toe.

"No. You are no better and no worse than Ruth. You both deserve care and respect. Everyone does. I can't say anything that can make you like anyone who is different from you. Only you can find that in yourself. Go home. All of you. I shall not mention this to Miss Stanley—not this time. But know this, Gertrude, I know about you. If I hear any more accounts of you bullying anyone, I shall be sure Miss Stanley is made aware of it. And, you, Sophie, will remember that violence begets violence. If it wasn't a waste of valuable paper, I would have you write lines to that effect. Now go."

We left the school as quickly as we could. Gertrude gave us one more poisonous glare and turned towards Penge. Marina and I headed for home.

Marina poked me in the ribs, grinning mischievously.

"So when we get back to the twenty-first century, are you going to tell Miss Pratt you decked her mother?"

I laughed uneasily, hoping that slugging Gert hadn't made matters worse.

CHAPTER 16

⟫⟫⟫ Saturday, November 2, 1940

Although Gert had given Pru, Ruth, Marina, and me a wide berth since the fight, I could still feel her eyes when we passed, but she looked away if I glanced in her direction. She never came close to us and never spoke to us. I should have been glad.

But how could I feel glad when I could see how desperately lonely she was? She didn't appear to have any friends—certainly not at school, anyway. Maybe, like me, she withdrew into a dream world. In my dream world, I was pretty and self-assured; maybe Gert had a dream world where she was adored. I sighed. I hoped so.

Quigs hooted with laughter as I walked smack into a lamppost.

"Blimey, Marina wears the glasses, but you're the one who's as blind as a bat. If you walk into things in the daylight, it's just as well Esther and Henry don't allow you out at night."

I grinned. It was good to hear Quigs laugh, even if it was at my expense. He'd been very quiet since two of his school friends had been killed on Wednesday night.

The six of us—Quigs, Marina, Bert, Pru, Ruth, and I—had been to the pictures, and were walking around Penge on a quest for adventure. Penge was becoming a depressing place where blackened shells of houses exposed their guts to the street. People's private lives—an unmade bed, a cupboard with the door hanging off, strips of flowery wallpaper fluttering in the breeze—were laid bare for all to see.

"The war isn't fun any more, is it Soph?" Quigs whispered, nodding at an old man sitting hunchbacked on the remains of his home, methodically pulling the petals off a solitary chrysanthemum.

I shook my head. "So do you want to go home now?"

Quigs' face hardened. "Back to the twenty-first century? Never. Come on; let's catch up with the others, before they think we're in love or something."

"Gross. Come on—race you!"

Pru pointed to a figure scrambling over a mountain of bricks. "Look—is that Gert? What on earth is she up to?"

"Probably scavenging," Quigs said. "Looking for stuff to sell, maybe."

"I don't think so. She seems to be digging for something." Pru raised her voice. "Gert! What are you doing over there?"

"Mind your own business."

Pru was not about to give up. "Gertrude Pratt! Tell me what you're looking for!"

"I said, mind your own business. And be quiet. I'm trying to listen," Gert said.

Listen for what? I clambered over the ruins to Gert.

Gert spun around. I grabbed her arm as she staggered and nearly slipped. She angrily shook off my hand. Then I heard the sound, too. From under the rubble, came the faint whimper of an animal, scared and in pain.

"It's not as loud as it was," Gert muttered. "I've got to get it out or it'll die."

"But how did you know it was here?" I asked, falling to my knees and starting to shift the bricks.

Gert shrugged. "When you're by yourself, you can hear things."

I turned to the others. "Come on! There's a dog stuck down there."

We carefully sifted through the pile of bricks, roofing tiles and wood, working slowly and methodically to avoid a cave-in. For more than an hour, we clawed away at the rubble with our bare hands. Our fingers and shins were cut to shreds. There was a lot to be said for the jeans I would have been wearing in my own time, I thought.

Gert struggled to shift a bathroom sink.

"Hey! Jew Girl!" she called. "Give me a hand with this."

Ruth clambered over to her, saying with quiet dignity, "My name is Ruth. A Jew is *what* I am; Ruth is *who* I am."

"Yeah. Just help me—lift—this."

Grunting, they heaved the sink out of the way.

Gert fell to her knees. "We're through! I can see the dog. If I can get down there, I can lift it out."

Bert peered through the hole. "Or you might bring the whole pile of rubble down on you. You'd be buried alive. Keep digging; we'll make the hole as big as we can. If we can make some sort of slope down there, it would be easier to get in and out than if it's a straight drop."

A thin, soaking drizzle was falling and the light was fading by the time we could safely reach the little terrier. Gert scrambled down and picked up the shivering animal.

"Ow! It bit me!"

"It's probably broken its leg or something," I called down. "Be careful, and try to stay away from its mouth."

Quigs and Bert reached down and hauled Gert out of the pit. She refused to let go of the dog, which had buried its head in her cardigan, quivering.

"Now what?" I asked. "We should really take it to a vet. I have an idea, we'll ask Esther to have a look at it for us. I wonder what happened to the people who lived here. I hope they're not still down there."

Marina wiped the rain spots from her glasses, saying, "Come on. We'd better get home quickly. It'll be dark soon, and I don't want to be staggering around in the blackout without a torch. Gert, won't your mum be getting worried about you?"

"Worried? About me? Don't be stupid. Worried that no one'll be there to feed the lodgers, maybe. Worried that no one'll be there to keep the boiler going, definitely. But worried about me? Don't make me laugh."

Marina stopped an air-raid warden hurrying down the road.

"Excuse me! That house over there—what happened to the people?"

"Why do you want to know?" he asked suspiciously.

"We've dug a dog out of the rubble and we were thinking—we were worried—"

"Oh, I see. Got Tizer out, eh? Is he all right? The people were in the shelter when the house was hit on Tuesday, I think it was. They're okay; I think they've gone down to relatives in Devon. Reckon they thought the dog was killed when the house came down. Don't know when they'll be back. What are you going to do with him?"

"I'm keeping him," Gert said fiercely. "They left him. He's mine."

"All right, miss. I'm not trying to take him from you. But get a move on. It's nearly dark, and the raids could start soon."

"Look, I'd better run," Pru said. "My mother will be frantic. Ruth, you live near me. I'll walk you home. Will the rest of you be all right to get home by yourselves?"

"Of course we will," Bert replied scornfully. "Don't need a blooming prefect to hold our hands. Come on, Gert. Let Mrs. Quigley have a look at old Tizer."

"No, no, I'm going home and taking Tizer with me."

"And what's your mother going to say when she sees that dog? She'll chuck him out quicker than you can say Jack Robinson. Let Mrs. Quigley check him over and I'll take care of him for you at the school," Bert promised.

"No." Gert clutched Tizer so tight he squealed loudly. "No. He's mine. I've never had anything before. He's mine, d'you hear?"

Clasping Tizer to her chest, she took to her heels and disappeared into the gloom.

❱ ❱ ❱

I was leaning into the deep bath, trying to coax the last of the brick dust—well, brick mud—down the drain when I heard a knock on the front door. My head jerked up at the sound of Gert's voice below. I bolted down the stairs as fast as I could.

"Please, sir," she said to Mr. Schmidt, "please could you ask Mrs. Quigley to have a look at my dog? He can't walk properly and he keeps crying and my mum says she'll get one of the boarders to kill him."

Esther bustled into the hall. "Hello, Gert! My goodness, what have you there?"

Gert repeated her tale to Esther.

"Well, I can't promise anything. I'm not a vet or a doctor, only a nurse. Dear me, he's in a state, isn't he? Come into the kitchen and let's see what's what. Put him on the floor and see if he can stand." She ran her hands gently over Tizer's legs and body. "It seems to be the front leg that's bothering him the most. I think it's broken. We need something to make a splint. Quigs, can you get the ruler from drawer and saw it in two? There's a saw in the cupboard under the stairs." She measured Tizer's leg and showed Quigs how long to cut the splints. "Make sure you sand the ends so there's no splinters. Marina, can you get a bandage and the ointment from the first aid box? Let's clean up those cuts and scrapes. You hold him in the sink, Gert, and I'll soap him up. Has he had anything to eat? Have *you* had anything to eat?"

Gert shook her head to both questions.

"Would you like some bread and gravy?"

Gert's eyes lit up for a second, then she replied: "No, no. That's all right. I'm fine."

But Mr. Schmidt was already heating up the leftover gravy. "A little for our four-legged friend, perhaps? And what else can we give him, Esther?"

"There's the chicken neck I used to make broth with. You can get the meat off that, if you like."

"Ah, yes! A dinner fit for a king."

Gert gaped at him.

"Why are you looking surprised, Gert? I, too, care for animals. Animals don't care where someone is from or if they're rich or poor. Give me an animal over some people, any day of the week."

Esther finished bandaging Tizer's leg, wrapped him in a towel, and handed him to Gert, who was still staring at Mr. Schmidt. Tizer wriggled and yipped at the smell of food. Heaven knows when he'd last eaten.

"Put that dog on the floor and eat up. Quickly. The planes are starting to go over."

It was a race to the finish as Gert and Tizer wolfed down their meals. The last mouthfuls disappeared as the wail of the siren started. Gert jumped to her feet, scooping Tizer into her arms.

"Thank you, Mrs. Quigley for fixing Tizer and for the food and everything. I've got to go."

"Gert, wait! Stay in our shelter with us; you may not make it home."

"It's all right. I'll duck into the school shelter. I need to see Bert. He said he'd look after Tizer for me. Reckon if I take him home, my mum really will have one of the boarders kill him. She doesn't have any spare food for him. And she'll say he's a waste of space. Thank you for everything."

Aside from her hateful tirades, that was the longest speech I'd ever heard from Gert. What a difference having a dog to love could make!

Without giving us a backward glance, Gert disappeared into the dark. I heard the side gate bang behind her and she was gone.

CHAPTER 17

))) Sunday Morning, December 15, 1940

Bombs banged and crashed all around me, changing into big bass drums in a brass band. A girl shouted my name as a mighty earthquake shook the ground.

"Wake up, Sophie! Wake up! Something's going on downstairs."

The banging in my dream came from the front door and Marina was the source of the shouting and shaking. You would have thought I'd be better at jumping out of bed at a moment's notice after all the practice I'd had, but I still couldn't find the sleeve of my robe and my left slipper.

Mr. Schmidt was opening the front door as I reached the top of the stairs. Three police officers—two men and a woman—stood on the doorstep.

"Mr. Smith? Mr. Henry Smith?"

"Yes. What is wrong? How can I help?"

"Perhaps you can come with us to the station, Mr. Smith. We would like to have a few words with you."

"Now? It is only six o'clock in the morning. Has something happened to one of my pupils?"

"No, Mr. Smith. You are being interned as an enemy alien under the Defense Regulations and Aliens Order Act of 1920."

I grabbed the newel post for support as blood pounded in my ears.

"Enemy alien?" said Esther, tying her robe as she came down the stairs. "What on earth are you talking about? He's not the enemy! He's Swiss, for heaven's sake. And unless you know something about the war that I don't, Switzerland is neutral. Or are you one of those who judge people based on their accent?"

The police officer shifted his feet uncomfortably as Esther glared at him, hands on hips. "Look, Esther, I'm sorry, but—"

"And don't you 'Esther' me, Percival Giles. If you're insulting my houseguest, then you'd better call me 'Mrs. Quigley,' because you're no friend of mine. And I would have thought you could wait until a more civilized hour to come here."

The female officer stepped forward and took Esther's arm. "Government guidelines state we should call early in the morning, so perhaps you could let us get on with our jobs. Now why don't you go and make yourself a nice cup of tea?"

I thought Esther was going to punch her. Mr. Schmidt touched Esther lightly on her shoulder.

"It's okay, Esther. Don't upset yourself. It's bad for the baby. I shall go with these officers, answer their questions, and be home by breakfast time. Don't worry."

A cold smile twisted Officer Giles' mouth. "I'm afraid you won't be home by breakfast. Perhaps it would be a good idea if you packed yourself a small suitcase. Change of clothes, shaving kit, that type of thing. And you'll probably be glad of a good book—a nice long one."

I sat down on the top stair as a clammy, dark fog slowly swallowed the hallway.

"Well, if you're taking Henry, you'll have to take me, too," Quigs' determined voice seemed so far away.

"No, son, not you. But the two girls will have to come."

"But the children are English. Why would you take them—and why only the girls?" Mr. Schmidt asked.

"We have our reasons. You'll find out. But the boy stays here. It's obvious he's Quigley's flesh and blood. You have ten minutes to pack."

"You can't do this!" Esther shouted, shaking loose from the policewoman's grasp. "You have no right! They're only children, and they're hardly what you'd call aliens. Or has the East End become a separate country overnight?"

Joseph appeared, crying and rubbing his eyes. Quigs picked him up and held him tight.

My legs shaking, I crept down the stairs.

"We don't have any suitcases," I whispered.

"Nine minutes."

Esther dug around under the stairs and brought out two suit-cases. Blinking furiously, she said, "You girls will have to share. It's probably just as well that you don't have much. Don't worry. I'll straighten this out." She held out her arms and Marina and I clung to her.

"Eight minutes."

Esther wheeled around. "Percy Giles, you're like a cross between Big Ben and the voice of the grim reaper. Stop this stupid count-down business and give them as long as they need. You always were a bully. But you might remember it wasn't that long ago I flat-tened your nose for you. Unless you want your fellow constables and your superior officers to find out just how recently that was and why it happened, show a little more compassion to my friends."

Quigs whistled softly in admiration.

Esther continued, "You three had better do as they say. Don't worry. I'll get you a lawyer to sort this mess out."

The other constable, who didn't look much older than me, said, "I'm sorry, but the government says enemy aliens aren't allowed to have a lawyer."

It was probably just as well that I didn't quite catch what Esther muttered under her breath because it didn't sound very complimentary.

"Come on, girls. I'll help you pack." Carrying the suitcases, Esther climbed the stairs, her back stooped with grief. At the top, she turned and said, "Hasn't this family contributed enough to this war? Isn't it sufficient that Fred gave his life? Why do we have to sacrifice our friends as well?"

I hung on to the banister like an old woman. My legs would hardly support me. This couldn't be happening.

Mr. Schmidt stood between Marina and me and put his arms around our shoulders.

"Don't worry, girls. We'll be all right."

Marina wiped the tears from her face with her hand.

"No we won't. You know it. We'll never get back now."

"Get back where?" said the policewoman, close behind us.

"The East End, where we came from. Where our parents died. Where we belong, because we obviously don't belong in Beckenham. If this is how you treat refugees from another part of London, I'd hate to think how you treat refugees from Europe."

The woman's eyes narrowed suspiciously.

"That's enough, young lady. Just pack your case."

She followed us into our bedroom where Esther was folding our clothes, tears streaming down her face. The policewoman walked around the room, looking in drawers, under the bed, in the closet.

"We'll make a thorough search of the house," she informed Esther, "so if you've ever seen anything like a radio or other communications device around, you'd better tell us now."

Esther straightened, rubbing her back.

"You really are amazingly stupid," she said calmly. "When I took these people in, everything they had was on their backs. I think I would have noticed if Marina had a radio stuffed down the front of her sweater or if Henry had signal flags sticking out of his back pocket. Or maybe you think that the Germans conveniently dropped a radio in our vegetable garden while they were dropping a few bombs on the rest of the area. Blimey, if our civil defense is in the hands of people like you, I fear for our country."

"Think seriously about anything you might have seen or heard. They're not as innocent as they look. We already have their camera."

)))

"Let me ask you one more time. What—is—your—name?"

"Inspector Thorne, let me tell you one more time. My name is Henry Smith."

"You could have picked a more original name that 'Smith.' But then, as it's close to your own name, I suppose it is easy to remember. Right, Henry Smith. Let me tell you your name. It's Heinrich Schmidt, isn't it?"

I gasped.

With the air of a magician producing a rabbit from a top hat, Inspector Thorne took Mr. Schmidt's Leica camera from his desk drawer.

"One of the more honest citizens of Penge found this in the corner of the air-raid shelter and brought it in to us. We waited for a month to see if anyone would claim it—after all, it's a very fine camera. If I'd dropped a camera like this, I'd certainly go to the local police station to see if it had been turned in. But no one came, so we developed the film to see if that would give us any clues as to the owner. When we took the film out, Mr. Smith, or you may prefer *Herr* Schmidt; we found your name written on the inside." He opened the camera. "See—Heinrich Schmidt. And the camera is made in Germany."

Mr. Schmidt shrugged. "What of it? Germans make excellent cameras. The war has only been on for a little over a year so I dare say more than a few citizens of England have old cameras made in Germany. And yes, my name is Heinrich Schmidt, but is that a crime? I'm from close to the German border in Switzerland; it makes sense I would have a German name. You may know of someone called MacDonald who is not from Scotland, and someone called O'Leary who has never even been to Ireland. You can't hang a man on account of his name."

"Maybe. Maybe not. But you can have reason for suspicion when you develop the film and find—not pictures of a children's party or a family picnic—but these!"

He triumphantly slapped a wad of photos on the desk. I drew in my breath and shut my eyes.

"Your young accomplice seems to know what these are. Look at her face. Guilt written all over it."

"Try fear, not guilt," Mr. Schmidt said sharply. "She's eleven, she's been awoken at some ungodly hour in the morning and dragged down to the police station on suspicion of being a German spy. What do you expect?" He paused for a second. "Those pictures are of a play we did in our last school about the Nazi regime. It was part of teaching the children about the issues involved in the war. I never thought education would be banned in England."

"I can't imagine the children's parents would be too pleased to see their children doing Nazi salutes, as they do in these pictures.

And look, here's one with you in it, accepting the salute. No, I don't believe that story. Surely you can do better than that."

Marina's eyes blazed green fire. "It's the truth! We're not Nazis. We're not German spies. Mr. Smith isn't an enemy alien—he isn't an enemy anything. What does it take to convince you?"

Inspector Thorne looked at Marina mockingly. "A good speech for someone so young. Tell you what, if your Mr. Smith can come up with a Swiss birth certificate, that would go a long way towards convincing me. Oh dear, I forgot it was conveniently lost in the air raid. I daresay the Swiss embassy should be able to help. Shall we contact them? But that's a job for tomorrow—Monday. For now, Mr. Smith will spend some time in a cell. As for you young ladies—I have been instructed to make sure you receive a good upbringing someplace where your obviously weak characters can be molded into those of decent British citizens. Somewhere where all your foolish, misguided notions of German supremacy can be laid to rest."

"But we don't have any notions of German supremacy!" I shouted. "Why won't you listen?"

"Anyway, it's best for everyone, even Mrs. Quigley. With Mr. Schmidt or Smith, whatever he wants to call himself, away, she won't have the benefit of his wage. Why should she have to support children who are not hers? What she does with the boy is up to her. He isn't in the pictures, so he obviously has no German sympathies. If she wants to keep him with her, that's fine. Surely you wouldn't want to cause Mrs. Quigley any hardship, not if you care for her as you say you do."

I fell silent.

"This afternoon, Policewoman Hargreaves will escort you to your new home in the country. A new home and a new life. Just what you need. Now say goodbye to Mr. Schmidt. You won't see him until after the war. With any luck, you'll never have to see him again."

CHAPTER 18

⟩⟩⟩ Sunday Afternoon, December 15, 1940

If I'd known then what I know now . . . If I'd known then what I know now . . .

The words pounded through my head to the rhythm of the train wheels.

If I'd known then what I know now, I certainly wouldn't have agreed to take part in that history assignment. I would have taken Mr. Martin's advice to leave the past alone.

I cleared a patch on the steamy window and pressed my nose against the glass. Not much to see. The smoky shroud from the locomotive added to the gloom of the wintry Kent countryside. I wondered where we were. All the station signs had been taken down in case the Germans invaded. I didn't even know where we were going. All Policewoman Hargreaves had told us was that we were to stay with a vicar in a village somewhere in Kent. I shut my eyes, thinking back over the events of the last few hours.

"I know the vicar personally," Hargreaves had said, as she marched us toward the train station. "You'll do well there if you behave yourselves. And you will behave. The vicar is extremely— strict, shall we say, which is a good thing. I think you two could do with some discipline."

Marina had stopped in her tracks at the bottom of Esther's street. "Miss Hargreaves, please may we be allowed to say goodbye to Esther, Joseph and Quigs? We have half an hour before the train is due to leave, and wouldn't you rather wait in comfort at Esther's house than in a drafty station waiting room? Please?"

"Oh, all right." Although her voice was grudging and impatient, it was clear that the thought of Esther's warm house compared favorably to the chilly station.

"You'll have to return that key," Hargreaves said sharply as Marina unlocked the front door.

Esther had been overjoyed to see us. "You're back! I knew they'd see reason. And how's Henry? Is he coming back soon, or does he have more questions to answer?"

I disentangled myself from Esther's hug.

"We're not back, not really. We're . . . we're being sent to live with a vicar in the country." I'd swallowed hard, determined not to cry. "Henry . . . Henry's still at the station in a cell. Oh, Esther, what are we going to do?"

My resolve crumbled and I dissolved into tears.

Quigs face darkened with anger. "They can't do that! They can't just lock someone up for not doing anything."

Hargreaves gave one of her mirthless smiles. "Oh yes we can. If you study the Defense Regulations, you'll find that on occasions such as this we can lock people up indefinitely. The girls' train leaves in less than half an hour. I only brought them by out of the kindness of my heart to say goodbye to you. So make the most of it."

Esther wiped her eyes and said, "Where are you taking the girls? You must tell me. I'm responsible for them."

"Not anymore, Mrs. Quigley. The government is responsible for them now. Don't worry; they'll be well cared for."

Esther made us sandwiches for the journey, even for Officer Hargreaves. As she handed them to us, she whispered, "I've put a ten shilling note between the wrappings of your sandwiches, so don't throw the paper out. Just stuff it in your pocket until you're alone."

The scrape of a match and the acrid smell of cigarette smoke pulled me back from the memory to the railway carriage. Hargreaves, sitting opposite Marina and me, smiled coyly at the sailor beside her. She took a cigarette from the silver case he held out to her, leaning close to him as he lit it. I opened the window in an attempt to get away from the smell of the smoke.

"Hey, shut that window," the policewoman ordered. "It's December, not the middle of July."

"She can't breathe because of your rotten smoke," Marina said. "And actually, neither can I. Can't you take your coffin nails out to the corridor?"

The sailor winked. "Come on. Let's go into the guard's car and smoke our cigarettes in peace."

"All right then. Being in the same compartment as these two Nazis is making me ill anyway," Officer Hargreaves said as she blew a smoke ring in our direction and followed the sailor out.

"Thank heavens for that," Marina muttered, waving the smoke away with her hand. "Don't know why it took them so long to invent no smoking laws." She poked me in my side and nodded at an elderly gentleman snoring loudly in the corner of the compartment. She whispered, "Do you think he's asleep—like *really* asleep?"

"Looks like it to me. Sounds like it too. No one could fake a snore like that, could they?"

"At the next station, we're getting out. Or even if the train stops between stations, we'll jump down. But either way, we're leaving."

"And do what? We don't even know where we are."

"Well, we know we're going away from London. So if we go the other way, we'll be going back to London, won't we? Come on, Soph!"

I pulled our suitcase down from the overhead rack.

"No, don't be silly. It would slow us down."

"I'm not going without this." I opened the case and took out the tray cloth my school friends had made. I tucked it into the pocket of my coat and stowed the case back on the rack as the train started to slow down.

"Sit down," Marina whispered. "Don't look suspicious. It's nearly dark so hopefully once we're outside, we won't be noticed."

The train slowly puffed to a halt. Marina put her hand on my arm as I went to open the door.

"Wait until the train starts to move again, and then get out quick. Okay . . . now!"

I cast an anxious glance at the man in the corner. He snored on. I opened the window, leaned out and unlatched the carriage door. We were out. Marina shut the door as gently as she could, although I doubted anything would have woken the snorer in the corner.

"Quick! Into the waiting room until the train's down the line a way."

After a minute, we stuck our heads out and looked around the deserted country station platform. The stationmaster was probably tucked up cozily beside his fire in the office. Off in the distance, I could hear a London-bound train chuffing closer. As the train drew into the station, we darted over the footbridge to the other platform and jumped into a compartment already occupied by two airmen. Amazingly, we knew one of them. My heart dropped.

Marina, though, was made of sterner stuff.

"It's Wing Commander Henderson, isn't it? Blimey, this is a coincidence!"

He stared at us through the gloom. "Aren't you the girls staying with Esther? What on earth are you doing out here?"

"Running away, actually. Not from Esther. We're running *to* Esther. You see, for some reason we were supposed to be evacuated to the countryside. Something about not being related to Esther. All I know is, we didn't want to go and Esther wasn't too happy about it either. But Sophie and I jumped ship at that last station and we're going back. You won't give us away, will you?"

I could tell by her voice that had the light been better, he would have been treated to the sight of her brilliant green eyes swimming beguilingly with unshed tears.

"No, of course I won't. It's the sort of thing I'd do in your place. Mind, if any of my men go AWOL, that's a different thing. Fitch, stick your head out and make sure the conductor isn't coming down the corridor. He struck me as a nosy sort of fellow, and I'll bet these two don't have tickets to Beckenham."

His companion obligingly looked down the corridor and quickly came back in.

"Blimey, he's gone into the compartment at the end of the car-riage. He's coming this way!"

"Curl up in the corners, girls. No, you sit over there. Put your feet up." He peeled off his greatcoat and draped it over me. I assumed Mr. Fitch did the same to Marina. I grunted as Wing Commander

Henderson leaned against me and started to snore loudly. From my itchy wool cocoon, I heard the compartment door open and after a couple of seconds, close again.

At last, I could breathe as Wing Commander Henderson lifted his weight and his coat off me.

"Are you okay? Didn't squash you, I hope. We'll have to change trains at Otford and Sevenoaks, so stay close to us."

I breathed a sigh of relief. The more times we changed trains, the harder we would be to follow.

"So what happened to that teacher fellow? Didn't he put up a fight to keep you?"

"Interned," Marina said. "They didn't believe he was Swiss, and he didn't have his birth certificate or passport. He sounds German, so to them he is German."

I closed my eyes and snuggled into the corner, hoping it would put off too many more questions. It worked.

The train from Sevenoaks was much more crowded than the other two, mostly with airmen and WAAFs heading back to Biggin Hill.

"Fitch and I are getting off at Knockholt. Will you two be okay to get to Beckenham from there? It's a straight run through and you should recognize Beckenham Junction station. Penge isn't far from there."

"We'll be fine," Marina assured him, sounding a lot braver than I felt. "If we're not sure where we are, well, we can ask, can't we?"

"Give my regards to Esther," Commander Henderson said, shutting the carriage door. "Take care and don't get lost."

My eyes stung as our two rescuers disappeared into the crowd of airmen.

"We won't get off in Penge. If they know we've escaped—and by this time, they must—that's where they would expect us to go."

"Marina, what are we going to do when we get to Penge? We can't go back to Esther's."

Marina sighed. "I wish I knew, Sophie, but I have no idea. No idea at all."

❱ ❱ ❱

Blending into a small group of people at Beckenham Junction station, we were safe and insignificant. We kept our faces averted as we walked calmly—well, outwardly calmly—past the stationmaster, out of the station and into the street.

I heaved a sigh of relief and linked my arm through Marina's. "So far, so good. What do you suppose Bert will think when we show up on his doorstep?"

Marina pulled her torch out of her coat pocket and shone the narrow beam down at the ground. "With his deadpan expression, we never know what he's thinking. I shouldn't think now will be any different. I hope his parents won't answer the door. Although, I really can't see them turning us in since they seem to have a rather relaxed attitude towards the law. I've never known anyone who gets as much stuff off the back of lorries as they do."

We trudged on in silence. A few planes went over but fortunately, the air-raid siren remained silent.

After a good forty-five minutes, we knocked on Bert's door. He stepped outside, quickly shutting the door behind him.

"What took you so long?"

"Well, you try escaping from the police and getting back to Penge from the wilds of Kent, and see how quickly you do it," I said.

"Well, you're here now. Go and hide in the shelter and I'll spring Mr. Smith for you."

I stared at him. "Spring Mr. Smith? How on earth are you going to do that? He's stuck in the cells at the police station, you know."

"Yes, I know that. I wouldn't be a good caretaker's son if I didn't know a thing or two about locks, would I? Get a move on. You don't have all night."

"I thought you didn't worry about time."

"Normally, I don't. Tonight, I do. Now move it!"

❱ ❱ ❱

I pushed my fist hard against my stomach, trying to stop its hungry, growling protests. In my head, the seconds ticked by on a huge mental grandfather clock.

"Suppose there's a raid, Marina? Suppose Bert gets caught? Suppose Henry's already been moved? Suppose—"

For the first time ever, Marina sounded annoyed with me. "Oh, Sophie, shut up, do! Don't keep supposing. From now on, we'll just have to take each second as it comes."

The door burst open. I snapped off the torch and huddled close to Marina in the corner.

"Girls, are you down there?" Mr. Schmidt whispered hoarsely.

We were plunged into darkness as the door banged shut.

To my horror, I heard the ghastly, familiar sound of Mr. Schmidt tumbling down the stairs and landing with a thud on the concrete floor below.

...What I Know Now

I turned the torch back on and we hurried over to where Mr. Schmidt lay beside the stairs, a crimson puddle by his head.

Not again.

"A.B.C," I said. "Airway, breathing, circulation. I learned it in first-aid class."

My head jerked up and I stared at Marina. I returned my attention to Mr. Schmidt and carried on mechanically, checking his breathing.

"Marina, help me put him in the recovery position. Unless he's broken his neck. We'd better make a neck collar out of a newspaper, just in case."

Once again I stopped. This was too weird.

"Sophie, stay here. I'm just going to check—"

Marina hurried up the stairs and flung open the door. Brilliant sunshine flooded the shelter.

Sunshine—on a dreary December night.

"I'll be right back," I whispered stupidly to the unconscious Mr. Schmidt and charged up beside Marina.

The bright sunlight dazzled me after the gloom of the shelter. I closed my eyes briefly and reopened them, grabbing the door for support as the world churned around me. The school window frames were painted white, not brown. There were no criss-crosses of brown tape on the panes. Instead of sandbags, a huge mound of drying London clay was piled by the entrance.

We were home.

Mr. Schmidt came up behind us. "What's going on? I must have banged my head too hard again. Maybe I'm dreaming."

"No, sir," I said softly. "You're not dreaming. We're home. But where's Quigs? Surely we can't have left him behind."

"How am I going to explain his disappearance to his parents?" Mr. Schmidt flinched as he touched his head. "Does anyone have a handkerchief? It's only a graze, I think, but it seems to be bleeding a lot."

Marina dug in her pocket and drew out a hankie. I pulled the tray cloth from my own pocket, and carefully unfolded it. My eyes blurred as I gently touched the stitching. Some of the girls who worked on it would be dead by now, 'died of natural causes,' as they would say on the news. Old age. Yet only a day ago, they'd been twelve.

A familiar voice dragged me back to the present.

"Leave the past alone, I said. But oh no, you had to go down the shelter. Had to delve into the past. And look where it got you."

"Mr. Martin, where's Quigs? Why didn't he come back?"

"He didn't come back because it was right for him to stay in 1940. He belonged there. You didn't."

Mr. Schmidt broke in. "But how are we to tell his parents we lost him somewhere in time? That's worse than leaving a child behind on a school trip."

"Oh, don't worry about that. He was never born."

We stared at him.

"If you don't believe me, go into the school and check the registers. Look at the school pictures. He won't be there."

In the school, Marina and I ran to the glass cabinet where important notices for parents were displayed. In pride of place was a picture of the school football team, of which Quigs had been the captain. The rest of the team was there, but the captain was Jane McIntyre. I made a face. Jane wasn't that good. My eyes dropped down to the picture of our graduating class. No Nathan Quigley.

We walked slowly back to the two men.

"He's right, Henry," said Marina. "Quigs isn't in the picture. But why wasn't he born?"

Mr. Martin's pale blue eyes clouded over. "Like I said, you shouldn't muck about with the past and the future." He pointed down the path to a tall, silver-haired man striding towards us. "If anyone can tell you why Quigs wasn't born, it's him."

Despite his age, the man walked with a spring in his step. He jauntily swung a brass-handled cane, occasionally prodding a bush with it.

Quigs.

"See, I told you I wasn't going back, didn't I?" He held out his hand to Mr. Schmidt, gesturing towards his forehead. "Hello, sir. Did you have a nice trip?"

"Ha! There is more of my blood on the floor of that shelter than there is in my body, I think. What's with the cane? You don't appear to need it."

"No, I don't; but it's rather cool, isn't it? Good for poking people with."

"What, like your old friends at school?" I asked.

He laughed. "Yeah. I nearly tripped Steve Bigley last week in the park. Pretended I was asleep on a bench and stuck out my cane as he walked by. You should have seen his face. It's quite fun sometimes, knowing all the kids without having been born. And all they see is an old man, not someone they should know."

"So why weren't you born?"

Quigs sighed and shook his head, a dark cloud crossing his face. "I wasn't born because . . . because Joseph died. It seemed someone had to die. Why does someone always have to die?" His defiant tone was that of the young, twenty-first-century Quigs.

After a pause, he continued, "When you went back, time shifted again. You went to the twenty-first century, the rest of us went back again to September fifteenth, nineteen forty. I went through everything all over again, but without you. I lived with Esther, went to this school and rode out to Biggin Hill with Bert. Fred came and visited Esther, just like before, but this time we knew how long we had to keep him there. When Henderson came to pick Fred up, I kept them talking in the house for five minutes while Bert took the rotor arm out of the engine. Of course, they quickly spotted the problem, but they couldn't find the rotor arm as Bert had run off with it. By the time they got back to Biggin Hill, they'd missed the initial scramble. They went up about an hour later, but by that time, history had changed. Fred lived."

Marina and I jumped up and down, shrieking.

"You did it, Quigs! You saved Fred's life."

"Yeah, Soph, I saved Fred's life. But Joseph was so enamored with his heroic, devil-may-care father, that he joined the Air Force when he grew up. His . . .his plane crashed on a training flight. He was only twenty years old."

His face twisted with anguish.

"Do you know what it's like knowing you're responsible for the death of your own grandfather?"

"No, Quigs," Marina said. "You're not responsible for his death. You're responsible for Fred living. Surely you can't regret that."

"Of course I don't. But sometimes I ask myself, if I'd had to choose who would live and who would die, what would I have done? I've never answered that question."

Mr. Schmidt put his hand on Quigs' shoulder. "You can't answer that question, Quigs. No one could, and it isn't fair to even ask it. You did what you had to do. So, bring us up to date on what has happened to everyone."

"Esther had a little girl called Sophie Marina. She said she kept dreaming about two girls, one called Sophie and the other called Marina. I never told her that it wasn't a recurring dream, that she really knew you. She wouldn't have believed me, anyway. Her daughter married and moved to Canada in 1964. Fred stayed in the Air Force for a while, and then took a job with an aerospace company as a test pilot. I bought the house from them twenty-five years ago when they retired to Cornwall. Fred died in 1995. Esther's still alive. She's over ninety. Ruth and I—oh yes, I married Ruth—made the dining room into a bedroom for Esther and she's living in her old house again. She's frail, but her mind is as clear as a bell."

"And what about Pru and Gert?" I asked.

"Pru didn't make it, I'm afraid." Mr. Martin said, his eyes as grey and as cold as the North Sea. "A doodle bug—you know, those pilotless flying bombs—got her in 1944."

No. Not kind, jovial Pru. She should have been a jolly field hockey teacher or a sergeant major. Not dead. Not Pru.

"What about Gert?" I whispered, my misery twisting like a knife in my stomach.

The brightness came back to Mr. Martin's blue eyes. "Ah, Gert. You could write a book about Gert. Here she comes with our daughter, Trudy. Now that times have changed, Trudy is known as Miss Martin, not Miss Pratt. Your don't want to go calling your head teacher by the wrong name. Don't look so astonished. It all started with Tizer. But like I said, it's a long story. One thing I do want to say before they get here—fill in that hole. No one must ever go down in that shelter again. *Ever.* Do you hear me?"

We picked up the shovels leaning against the mound of clay and started back-filling as quickly as we could.

Miss Pratt's—no, make that Miss Martin's—disappointed voice was right behind me. "Oh, you're filling it in again. What happened? And Mr. Schmidt, what on earth happened to your head?"

Mr. Schmidt touched his wound. "This is the reason we're filling in the excavation, Miss Martin. The shelter is too dangerous to enter. The stairs are gone and the concrete is crumbling. We don't want any more accidents."

"Don't know why anyone would want to go down there anyway," Gert grumbled.

I grinned. She certainly sounded the same.

Gert peered at Mr. Schmidt, Marina, and me.

"Do I know you? You look so familiar."

Marina replied, "You've probably seen us on the High Street."

Gert sniffed. "Maybe." She turned to Mr. Martin. "So are you coming to the supermarket with me, or what?"

"I'm coming, my dear. Quigs, will you walk with us?"

"Certainly. I have to pick up some items for Ruth."

The two women walked on ahead.

"Tamp that down tight," Quigs said to Mr. Schmidt. "And when you're done, do you want to meet Bert and me in the pub for our Saturday lunchtime pint? Sorry, girls, you're too young."

If Quigs hadn't been an elderly gentleman, I would have heaved a clod of clay at him.

"It would be a pleasure. But I'm afraid I only have 1940's money."

"Oh, I'll stand you a pint. I think it's the least I can do."

Laughing, Quigs and Mr. Martin hastened to catch up with the ladies.

I felt in my pocket for a hankie and pulled out my sandwich wrapper from yesterday, sixty-two years ago. The ten-shilling note was still there, amongst the stale breadcrumbs. Through a veil of unshed tears, I saw Mr. Schmidt leaning on his spade, his face barren and desolate.

"Sir, are you okay? Aren't you glad to be back?"

"Yes, of course I am, Sophie. Coming back was the right thing to have happened." His despondent tone belied his words. After a pause, he continued, "But you're not the only dreamer, Sophie. And if I'm honest with myself, Quigs isn't the only person who wanted to stay."

"Because of Esther?" I whispered.

"Esther," he repeated softly, a faint, sad smile touching his lips. "Esther was a remarkable woman. As you will be one day, Sophie." He picked up his spade. "Come on. Keep shoveling."

❭ ❭ ❭

If I'd known then what I know now . . .
I'd do it all again.

End

Acknowledgements

I'd like to thank Doris Pullen, John Mead and Janice Sculley for their contributions to *The Secret Shelter*. I'm especially grateful to Bob Billinghurst for sharing his rich, heart-warming reminiscences of school life in wartime Penge. Thank you, all.

About the Author

Born in England, Sandi LeFaucheur bounced across the Atlantic several times before settling in South London. As a secretary in the school in which *The Time Shelter* takes place, Sandi was intrigued by the air-raid shelter buried beneath the front lawn. As she couldn't excavate it, she decided to write about what could be down there, and what might befall anyone foolish enough to enter…

Sandi, her husband, teenage son, and elderly Golden Retriever bounced one final time across the Atlantic in 2000. They now live in a small town in the rolling hills of Southern Ontario.